The Lost Treasure
of Casa Loma

Books by Eric Wilson

The Tom and Liz Austen Mysteries

Also available by Eric Wilson

The Lost Treasure of Casa Loma

A Tom and Liz Austen Mystery

by

ERIC WILSON

HarperCollins*Publishers*Ltd

For my friends in England
The Tinkers and Brian Atkinson
Tim Oldroyd and Curt Noel

The Lost Treasure of Casa Loma
© 1979 by Eric Wilson Enterprises, Inc.
Illustrations copyright © 2005 by Susan Tooke. All rights reserved.
Logo photograph by Heath Moffatt@ 2003 eweInc

Published by Harper*Trophy*Canada™, an imprint of HarperCollins Publishers Ltd

First published by General Paperbacks: 1982 This Harper*Trophy*Canada mass market paperback edition: 2005

Harper*Trophy*Canada™ is a trademark of HarperCollins Publishers

HarperCollins books may be purchased for educational, business, or sales promotional use through our Special Markets Department.

HarperCollins Publishers Ltd
2 Bloor Street East, 20th Floor
Toronto, Ontario, Canada
M4W 1A8

www.harpercollins.ca

Library and Archives Canada Cataloguing in Publication

Wilson, Eric, 1940-
    The lost treasure of Casa Loma / Eric Wilson.

"A Tom and Liz Austen mystery".
ISBN-13: 978-0-00-639544-7 / ISBN-10: 0-00-639544-9
I. Title.
PS8595.I583L68 2005   JC813'.54   C2005-902442-9

OPM 9 8 7 6 5 4 3 2 1

Printed and bound in the United States

As in his other mysteries, Eric Wilson writes here about imaginary people in a real landscape. Find Eric Wilson at www.ericwilson.com

cover design by Richard Bingham
cover and chapter illustrations by Susan Tooke
logo photograph by Heath Moffatt © 2003 eweInc.

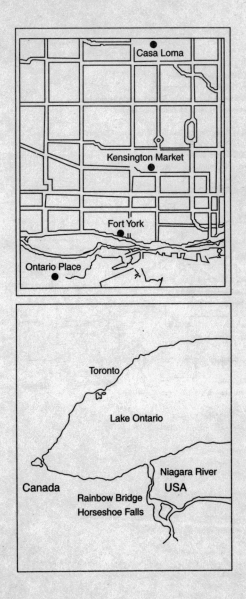

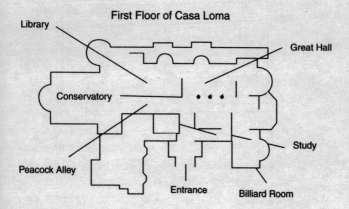

First Floor of Casa Loma

Library

Great Hall

Conservatory

Study

Peacock Alley

Entrance

Billiard Room

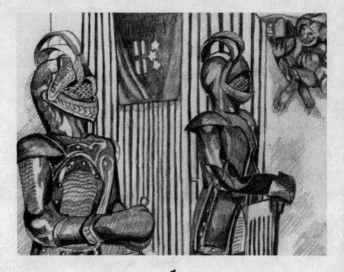

1

"We fear it was murder."

The butler's gloomy face was lit by a flash of lightning. "But please come in. Mr. Winter will tell you all the details about Sir Nigel's disappearance."

Tom shivered with excitement as he stepped into Casa Loma, a castle in the heart of Toronto. He put down his backpack and followed his sister Liz and their Uncle Henry to the castle's Great Hall.

A log fire roared, throwing an orange light on suits of armour and crossed lances on the walls.

"Welcome to Toronto, Mr. Austen." A handsome dark-haired man came forward to shake Uncle Henry's hand. "I'm Vince Winter, a close friend of Sir Nigel's."

After the introductions were over, Uncle Henry went to the enormous fireplace to warm his hands.

"This is a sad occasion. I was very fond of Sir Nigel."

Vince looked thoughtfully into the flames. "We don't know that he's actually dead."

"What happened?"

"I'll tell you in just a minute. First, if I may, let me introduce Sir Nigel's private secretary."

A young woman in a wheelchair came across the Great Hall toward them. "I'm Tia Nightingale, Mr. Austen."

"Please, Tia, first names only."

She smiled. "That's a nice idea. But you may get objections from the new butler, Smythe. He's only been at Casa Loma a few days, and seems a bit stuffy."

Tom glanced toward a distant corner of the Great Hall, where the butler stood under a carving of an evil-eyed jester. Had he heard Tia?

Vince motioned to Smythe. "Sherry, please, and Cokes for Tom and Liz."

"Very good, sir."

Vince led Uncle Henry through a doorway. "This is the library. Let's have our sherry in here, while I tell you as much as I know about Sir Nigel's disappearance."

Smythe appeared with a silver tray, and passed around the drinks. Tia sipped hers cautiously, then nodded. "I'm pleased this is actually sherry. Yesterday Smythe served us brandy by mistake."

Tom thanked the butler for his Coke, and accepted a tiny sandwich served by a pretty maid named Irene. Then he waited impatiently for details of Sir Nigel's mysterious disappearance, which had brought Uncle Henry to Casa Loma. Tom and Liz had been staying with their uncle when the news had arrived, and they had been excited by the prospect of accompanying him to Toronto.

But, before anyone could speak, a thin man of about sixty came into the library and approached Uncle Henry. "May we have a word in private, Mr. Austen?"

"We don't have secrets out West, where I come from. Please speak your piece."

The thin man swallowed nervously, and glanced toward Smythe. "My name is Hatfield, and I am Sir Nigel's personal servant—his valet. I have been in his service for many years now. Is it correct you are taking over Casa Loma?"

Uncle Henry nodded, and his glasses caught the light. "Sir Nigel is my cousin. If he can't be found, I will inherit the castle."

"Then, sir, I must warn you something is terribly wrong! Some of the new servants, including Smythe, don't even know their jobs. But it's the stables I must tell you about. I . . ."

At that moment the lights went out. Startled cries sounded in the room, then Smythe's reassuring voice was heard.

"The storm must have blown down the power lines," he said. "I'll fetch some candles."

Suffocating darkness filled the library, and Tom's nerves prickled with tension as the minutes passed. Why was Smythe taking so long?

At last a match flared into life and the yellow light of several candles cut the darkness, revealing the shadowed faces of the assembled company.

"Well, Hatfield?" Uncle Henry said, looking around for the valet. "What were you saying?"

"He's not here, Unc," Liz said.

"But where has he gone?" said Irene, the pretty maid. On her face was total astonishment.

"Let's not worry about Hatfield now," Vince said. "I was about to tell you what happened to Sir Nigel. Come along, and I'll show you the room where he disappeared." Picking up a candlestick, Vince led the way to a long dark hallway. "This is called Peacock Alley. Over here is the door to Sir Nigel's study. Nothing in it has been moved since he disappeared."

Opening the door, Vince stepped into the study. Then he gasped. "Oh no! It can't be!"

The horror in his voice made Tom's hair stand on end. Stepping closer, he looked into the study. Sprawled in the room, the twisted features of his face yellow in the candlelight, was Hatfield.

2

"Everyone get back!"

Vince slammed the study door and gestured to the maid. "Irene, go phone the police!"

"Yes, Mr. Winter."

"I insist we all wait together until the cops arrive."

Tom nodded his head in agreement as he glanced around at the other faces in the yellow candlelight. Had one of them attacked Hatfield and then dragged the valet to the study while the lights were out? Obviously Uncle Henry and Liz were not involved, but that still left several other suspects.

"Mr. Winter," Irene called, hurrying back toward them along Peacock Alley. "The phone is dead, so I can't call the police."

"Surely the storm hasn't affected the phone as well?"

"Perhaps someone cut the line. Could that be possible?"

"That's *very* possible, Irene." For several long moments Vince gazed thoughtfully at the young maid, until finally she dropped her eyes. "Well, I'd better drive to a police station and make a report. But, first, we'll have to find out what happened to Hatfield."

Tom edged closer, his heart beating rapidly as he watched Vince open the study door and look inside.

The room was empty.

"That's impossible!" Tom stared into the study. "There's only the one door, and no windows!"

Suddenly the lights came back on and everyone crowded into the room, staring at the place where they had seen Hatfield's body only moments before.

"We can't *all* be crazy!" Vince tried to smile. "I'm sure the police will find an explanation. But, first, let's go back into the library so I can tell you about Sir Nigel."

Tia shivered as she turned her wheelchair to leave the study. "A second mysterious disappearance within a few days. I think I'll look for another job."

"Please don't," Uncle Henry said, walking beside her into the library. "I'd be lost, trying to run this place alone."

Vince sat down and stretched his long legs, then glanced at his fancy watch. "I'm sorry, it's getting late, but I do want you to hear about Sir Nigel."

"Yes," said Uncle Henry. "We'd better hear quickly, before someone else disappears." No one returned his faint smile. They were all too nervous.

Tia leaned forward in her wheelchair. "As you

know, Sir Nigel Brampton purchased Casa Loma a year ago, after retiring here from Britain. The castle cost a mint, but Sir Nigel had earned millions from oil and gold."

Vince smiled. "Millions? I'd have said jillions, or maybe zillions."

"Sir Nigel was fascinated by Casa Loma and tried to find out as much history as he could. One unusual thing he learned was that the original owner was so horse-crazy that he had false teeth made for a favourite charger, but that's not—"

"Excuse me," Liz said. "I'm a horse freak, too. Did the false teeth work?"

"I don't know," Tia answered, smiling. "Anyway, one day Sir Nigel discovered an old coded document. When he broke the code, it led him to a cache of hidden diamonds."

"Diamonds! How fabulous!"

"Fabulous is right. I saw them once, shortly before Sir Nigel hid them again, and they were gorgeous. Tiny, radiant perfection."

Uncle Henry frowned. "You say he *hid* them again?"

"Yes. Sir Nigel wouldn't trust a safety-deposit box, so he found a new hiding-place in Casa Loma."

Vince gulped down the last of his sherry. "Shortly afterwards, I was introduced to Sir Nigel by Tia, and we became close friends. I urged him to put the diamonds in a bank, but he refused."

Tia shook her head. "That was a mistake. The police are convinced that criminals are behind Sir Nigel's disappearance. They're after the diamonds."

"Exactly what happened?" Liz asked.

"A week ago, Sir Nigel was working in the study. A maid had just taken him a cup of tea when she heard a terrible cry. Rushing back to the study, she found Sir Nigel lying face-down across his desk, apparently dead or at least unconscious."

Vince shuddered with the memory. "I was a weekend guest of Sir Nigel's at the time. When the maid raised the alarm, I rushed to the study and . . ."

"Yes?"

"And the study was empty."

"Just as it was with Hatfield!"

"Exactly. Sir Nigel disappeared into thin air. Not one word has been heard from him since."

For a moment no one spoke. Tom glanced at Liz, wondering what his sister thought about the strange events at Casa Loma. Suddenly there was a loud crash somewhere in the castle. Tom and Liz both stared toward the sound.

Vince smiled. "Don't worry, Casa Loma doesn't have ghosts. Sometimes the wind slams a door."

"What about that horrible creaking?" Liz asked.

"That's only the teak floors."

"Are you sure? It sounds more like a pack of zombies roaming around."

Vince smiled, then turned to Uncle Henry. "And so, as Sir Nigel's closest relative, you have been summoned from Winnipeg to look after Casa Loma. Should Sir Nigel not be found, the castle will be yours."

A mournful grandfather clock tolled midnight.

Uncle Henry ran his hand nervously through his hair.

"Sir Nigel had better be found. This castle gives me the creeps."

* * *

The next morning Tom felt groggy. He hadn't slept well, despite the luxury of a massive bed in the Round Room, which had once been occupied by the Duke of Windsor.

Tom went down to the Great Hall in search of breakfast, and found Liz already there combing her dark hair in front of a gold-framed mirror.

"Guess what?" she said happily. "The shower in my suite has perfumed water."

"My bathroom's so big, I could use a bike to get around. But there's only a bathtub."

"One of the servants told me Sir Nigel's private suite has a fabulous shower with six taps. Apparently Sir Nigel never bothered using it, but I'm sure no one would object if you tried."

Smythe appeared. "Breakfast is served, young sir and madam."

The butler's glum face was an upsetting reminder of Hatfield's disappearance the night before. The castle was spooky even in daylight; Tom and Liz followed Smythe into the breakfast room, where Uncle Henry was eating a huge serving of bacon and eggs while talking to the young maid, Irene.

"Good morning, kids! How'd you sleep?"

"So-so," Tom said, sitting down in a gigantic chair carved with sea serpents and dragons. "Have the police arrived yet?"

Uncle Henry shook his head. "Not yet. Vince drove down to make a report last night after you'd gone to bed. They'll probably be here later this morning."

"Great! I can't wait."

Uncle Henry smiled, looking a bit sheepish. "I hate to be a killjoy, but I've already planned your morning. You'll be with Irene. You've only got a week's spring holiday from school, so I figured you'd want to explore Toronto before you fly home."

Irene grinned at Tom and Liz. "How about us seeing a human scalp this morning?"

"Hey," Tom said. "That sounds all right!"

Just then, Tia entered the room in her wheelchair. "Planning to visit Fort York? I'd enjoy showing you round. Before my accident, I was a guide there."

"Then take the morning off," Uncle Henry said. "With Smythe and twenty-five servants, the castle should survive! Right, Smythe?"

The butler nodded solemnly. Dark circles under his eyes, and several shaving cuts on his chin, made him an unattractive sight this morning. Tom was glad Smythe wasn't going to Fort York with them.

* * *

The first sight of the fort was a Union Jack, being tossed by the cold, rainy wind. As they drove into the parking lot, they heard a cannon boom.

"Want some help?" Tom asked, as Tia wrestled her wheelchair out of Irene's car.

"No thanks, I'm used to this. I drive myself to work, using hand controls."

Tia wheeled the chair toward the fort, leaving two long tracks behind her on the muddy path. "During the War of 1812," she explained to Tom and Liz, "American forces invaded this area. Fort York was the headquarters of the British defenders."

Irene smiled. "These days, the American invaders are all tourists."

Tia smiled. "And some of us like Canada so much, we stay."

"Are you from the USA, Tia?"

She nodded. "Look, there's the Fort York guard, drilling with Brown Bess muskets. Aren't their red uniforms splendid?"

"Where's that scalp?"

"Follow me," Irene said, laughing.

The scalp—long black hair and a bit of skin attached to a wooden stretcher—was displayed inside a barracks. Then Tom and Liz followed the others to the fort's magazine to see a shot-oven. This, Tia told them, had been used for heating cannonballs to set enemy ships on fire.

Next, they went into the officers' kitchen, where an aproned girl was making cinnamon doughnuts over an open fire. Copper pots reflected the flickering flames, and the circles of sizzling dough made Tom's mouth water.

The girl gave each of them a doughnut, and Tom wandered outside eating his.

Hatfield was standing in the yard.

Tom nearly choked on his doughnut. He hurried toward the man.

"Hatfield! You're alive!"

The man's face went white when he saw Tom. He turned to the two small children at his side. "Go and find Granny. I'll be there in a minute."

When the children were gone, he looked at Tom. "O.K., so I'm Hatfield. What of it?"

"What happened last night? And what were you going to say about the stables?"

Hatfield glanced nervously at some passing people. "Just that the blacksmith was pounding cold iron. Now, please, leave me alone."

Hatfield started away, but Tom followed. "What happened to you after the lights went out?"

Hatfield's face was marked by tension. "Listen to me. They've threatened my family if I talk to anyone about Casa Loma. So please get away from me."

"*Who* threatened you?"

Hatfield stared at Tom with fear written on his face, then he hurried toward the parking lot. Puzzled, Tom watched him get into a car with a woman and the two young children.

After making a note of the car's licence plate number, Tom walked back toward the officers' quarters. He was greatly relieved to discover that Hatfield had not been murdered the night before, but he was completely mystified by the strange events that had happened at Casa Loma.

Speaking of the castle, what was all this about a blacksmith? Tom stopped to jot *blacksmith pounding cold iron* in his notebook, then continued on with a big smile on his face.

Excellent lead!

3

"Guess what?" Tom exclaimed, as the others came out of the officers' quarters. "Hatfield is alive!"

Tia was shocked. "You must be joking!"

"He was right here at Fort York, large as life and happy as a clam. Happy, that is, until I gave him the third degree and he spilled a clue that points me straight at a major suspect."

"A suspect? Who is it?"

"I shouldn't say, in case my man's innocent and I ruin his reputation."

Tia studied Tom's face thoughtfully. "I admire that." She wheeled her chair toward the parking lot. The others followed, and they were soon heading back to the castle.

The towers of Casa Loma were magnificent as they approached. "What a sight!" Liz said. "Unless the crooks have found them, the diamonds must be hidden in one of the castle's ninety-eight rooms. I wonder which one?"

Tia brushed back her thick curls. "Sir Nigel once teased me with a clue, but I couldn't figure it out."

"A clue! Please tell us."

"These were his exact words: 'It's the same place as pictures are sent, when they've made a mess of things.'"

"Weird."

* * *

Back at the castle, Tom and Liz found Uncle Henry in the billiard room. They told him about Hatfield, and he was equally puzzled by the man's strange behaviour. Although the police still had not arrived to investigate yesterday's events, the morning had been busy, and unpleasant, for Uncle Henry.

"The servants are complaining about Smythe, and threatening to quit if the former butler doesn't return."

"But where is the original butler?" Liz asked.

"No one knows. He left shortly after Sir Nigel disappeared, then Smythe came as his replacement. According to the other servants, Smythe is making a mess of things. They say he's incompetent."

"Why don't you boot him out?"

Uncle Henry made an unhappy face. "I tried to, Liz, but I just couldn't do it. I talked to Smythe, said he had to leave, and the poor man was so upset that I changed my mind. But I warned him he'll have to shape up or ship out."

Liz smiled. "Get on the ball, Smythe, or get on the boat."

"You bet!" Uncle Henry tried to look stern.

"Say, Unc, may we explore the castle's towers?"

Uncle Henry nodded, smiling. "Let's ask Smythe to take us. It might cheer him up."

* * *

Not long afterwards, they were climbing stairs which spiralled up inside a gloomy tower. Tom half expected to be attacked by bats, and was pleased to step out into the open air.

"Be careful," Smythe warned as they approached the stone rampart around the roof. "The rain has made it slippery up here."

"Far-out view," Liz said, looking at the city's famous CN Tower and the skyscrapers gleaming along the shore of Lake Ontario. "This was a great place to build a castle."

"Casa Loma is Spanish for 'house on the hill.' "

"Some house!"

Tom and Liz crossed over to the other side of the tower roof. Leaning over the rampart, they looked down at the red tiles and stone unicorns below.

"Those must be the stables," Tom whispered, pointing at a distant building. "Got time to investigate them?"

"Because of what Hatfield told you?"

"Yes. He said that—"

Suddenly there was a terrible cry. Whirling around, Tom saw Uncle Henry and Smythe struggling at the edge of the rampart. For an awful moment Tom thought Smythe was trying to push Uncle Henry over. Then he realized that in fact the butler had kept his uncle from falling. Tom ran to help, but before he reached him, Uncle Henry had managed to scramble back to safety.

"I almost fell! I leaned against the rampart and something slipped. Thank heavens, Smythe, that you were right beside me!"

A closer look revealed a loose stone in the rampart. Uncle Henry seemed satisfied that this had caused the nearly fatal accident, but Tom still kept a long way from Smythe as they descended the tower's narrow stairs.

"Let's try those stables," Tom whispered to Liz, when they were alone.

It was now pouring with rain and the water bounced off the road as Tom and Liz ran to the stables. "I'm soaked!" Liz wiped her foggy glasses. "We should have asked the chauffeur to drive us over."

Tom laughed. "This rich life suits you, Liz. Soon you'll be taking baths in milk."

Liz glanced into a feed room, but it was empty. Cobwebs were thick in the corners. "The stables must be . . . Yikes!"

A huge man appeared from around a dark corner. For a moment he stared at them with unsmiling eyes. "Get out of here," he said, gesturing menacingly with an enormous hand.

"Hey," Tom protested. "We want to see the stables." When there was no reply, he swallowed nervously and added, "Please."

"There's nothing to see. The horses are at winter quarters in the southern USA."

"We still want to look around," Tom said.

"Not a chance."

"Oh, well," Liz shrugged. "We'd better come back with Uncle Henry. You'll let your new boss look around, won't you?"

The man looked hostile. After a moment, he pointed down a dark passage. "Follow that and you'll find the horse stalls."

"Thanks."

Tom and Liz stumbled along the dark passage but it led to a blank wall. Returning, they heard the sound of metal ringing against metal and followed it to a large room containing two rows of enclosed horse stalls. Near a forge, a blacksmith—the same unfriendly man they'd seen earlier—was pounding a horseshoe on the anvil. Tom shivered, wishing there was a fire in the forge to warm the chilly air.

"Let's go," he shouted to Liz above the noise of the blacksmith's ringing blows.

As they reached the outside door, footsteps sounded from the dark passage and a man came out, carrying a tray of steaming food. It was the chauffeur who'd met them at the airport yesterday.

"Oh," he said. "You startled me! I, uh, brought my lunch over from Casa Loma. I like eating in private."

"How about a ride home after you've eaten?" Liz asked.

The chauffeur smiled, but a nerve twitched in his eyelid. "Afraid not, Miss. The limousine's parked at the castle."

"Oh, your clothes are dry, so I thought you must have driven over here."

The chauffeur mumbled something as he headed for the horse stalls. Outside, Liz turned her face to the rain.

"Did you notice the horses' names in gold on the doors of the horse stalls? I bet there's enough room inside those huge stalls for a horse to entertain several friends to tea."

"All I noticed was that blacksmith's arms. If the diamonds are hidden under the castle, he could just lift it up for us. I wonder why he lied about the location of the horse stalls?"

Tom had planned to question the blacksmith about what Hatfield had said concerning the stables, but one look at those muscles and the plan had evaporated. Embarrassed by this failure, and feeling miserable after the rain, he decided to drown his blues in a hot shower.

Remembering the fabulous shower in Sir Nigel's private suite, he headed there after receiving permission from Uncle Henry.

His footsteps were silenced by a thick carpet as he entered the suite. Then he stopped in surprise. Standing beside a table and holding a photograph in a silver picture frame was the maid, Irene.

She didn't notice Tom, and he didn't speak. After studying the photograph for a few moments, Irene put it down and turned toward the door.

"Tom! What a scare you gave me! I, um, I was checking that everything's O.K. in here."

Tom glanced toward the wooden bedstead, carved with forked-tongued serpents. "But this suite hasn't been used for a week."

Irene smiled, pushing her black hair away from her face. "You're right. Actually, I was walking past the room and saw the secret panel was open. I came in to close it, then noticed that photograph of Sir Nigel and your uncle."

"A secret panel! May I see it?"

Irene went to the fireplace. "There's a button hidden under the mantel. You just push it, and presto."

A thin panel beside the fireplace swung open, revealing narrow shelves holding books and papers. "Disappointed?" Irene smiled. "I bet you expected to see the diamonds."

"This secret panel hardly seems secret."

"You're right. All the servants know about it. But I wonder who opened it, and why."

When Irene had left, Tom went into Sir Nigel's bathroom. The marble walls were streaked with colours, and the many fixtures included a telephone linked to the castle's private phone system.

Dropping his clothes on the floor, Tom stepped into the shower. Six separate taps controlled the spray from silver rails which enclosed him. The hot, stinging water coming from all directions was so invigorating that Tom began to sing.

Perhaps in protest, the main pipe clunked loudly and the water died to a trickle. Tom was disappointed! Unable to get the water flowing again, he grabbed a fluffy towel and rubbed his hair until it stood up in red spikes.

Then Tom noticed that a tube of Sir Nigel's toothpaste had been cut neatly in half. The toothpaste had been squeezed out and hadn't yet hardened. It looked as if someone had suspected this was the hiding-place for the diamonds—someone who had very recently been in the bathroom.

A shiver passed through Tom. Close by in the castle there was someone, perhaps well known to Tom, who was behind the disappearance of Sir Nigel and the determined search for the diamonds.

But who?

4

Vince and Tom walked along a sidewalk, jostled by the shoppers crowding Toronto's Kensington Market. Vince had purchased a couple of Jamaican hot beef patties, and Tom was eating his while he tried to puzzle out a meat market sign reading *Grande Especial Carne de Porco*.

"Big special on pork chops, I guess. What language is that?"

"Portuguese. Toronto is home to people from all over the world, including yours truly. I'm from San Francisco."

Tom looked in the door of a music store, where music blasted and a straw-hatted clerk danced behind the counter. The boy gave Tom a friendly wave, inviting him to join in, but Tom shyly shook his head and hurried on.

A sweaty teenager came their way, trundling a cart loaded with red snappers on ice; as the fish passed, their huge, dead eyes seemed to stare at Tom. "They're as unpleasant a sight as the face on that Casa Loma blacksmith. There's something strange happening in the stables, Vince. I'm going to poke around there this evening."

"So you said earlier. And I repeat my warning: don't chance it."

Tom bent to rub the head of a mongrel sprawled in a doorway. "Why'd you move here from the USA, Vince?"

"I was offered a sportscasting job by a local TV station. I'm pleased to say the station's ratings are now huge. We're number one."

"Which sports?"

"You name it, I report it. Most of the pro athletes in town are close buddies of mine."

"Like who?"

"Dexter Valentine, for one."

"Dexter Valentine is your friend? I don't believe it!"

"Then why don't I prove it?" Vince crossed the narrow street. "Let's ring this doorbell, and see if Dexter's home."

Tom waited, doubtful that the famous shortstop for the Toronto Blue Jays baseball team would really open the door.

When he did, Tom's jaw fell open. He was still struggling for speech after he'd been introduced and they'd gone up a flight of stairs to an apartment overlooking the market.

"Liveliest view in town," Dexter said, leading them

onto the balcony. "Plus fresh fruit and vegetables, right on our doorstep."

Tom tried to think of an intelligent comment, but could only stare in awe at the man. He'd seen him so many times on television! His wife came onto the balcony carrying a baby, and Tom was introduced. The Valentines then produced some refreshments, and Tom gradually began to relax.

"This is delicious," he said, taking another bite of a crunchy, corn-meal fritter as he looked down at the market from the balcony.

Vince looked at his watch. "I should be heading for the TV station soon. Hey, Tom, how about you and Liz seeing tomorrow night's baseball game as my guests?"

"Fantastic!"

"Then, with the Valentines' permission, I'll use their phone to make the arrangements."

When Vince had left the balcony, Tom worked up the courage to ask Dexter Valentine how he liked being a star baseball player. The man laughed good-naturedly, and told some fascinating stories about life in professional baseball.

"The player under the most pressure is the pitcher, who's the focus of constant attention. When he has a bad game, and makes such a mess of things that another pitcher must take over, it's a long and unhappy walk to the showers."

"Wait a minute," Tom suddenly exclaimed. "That's it!"

"Huh?"

"Tia got it wrong! Sir Nigel didn't say 'pictures,' he said 'pitchers'!"

As the Valentines stared in amazement, Tom did a joyful jig around the balcony. Vince returned, and Tom blurted out, "Guess what? I know where the diamonds are hidden!"

Vince laughed briefly, but then looked thoughtful. "I believe you mean it." Tom grinned happily. "So? Where are they?"

"I'd rather not say, in case I'm wrong. But let's head for Casa Loma, and I'll test my theory."

"Hold your horses. We can't just leave in the middle of visiting the Valentines."

Tom choked back his disappointment as Vince sat down and accepted another cup of coffee from the Valentines, then explained to the puzzled couple why Tom was so excited. All three then did their best to get the secret out of Tom, but he just grinned and shook his head.

"What if I'm wrong? I'd look like a prize turkey."

Smiling, Vince stood up. "It's clear Tom can't be moved, and I must get going. One more phone call, and then we'll say good-bye."

Vince was gone some time, and Tom tried to calm his excitement while he bounced the gurgling baby in his arms. But at last Vince was ready to leave, and they were soon hurrying through the market. Tom barely noticed the delicious smells from bakeries and spice sellers in his eagerness to get back to the castle.

"Listen, Tom," Vince said, "I'm already late for an on-air interview with Jacques Savard, the ice hockey player. You'll have to take a streetcar to Casa Loma."

"Sure, Vince, and thanks. It was great touring the market and meeting the Valentines. Liz made a big mistake, deciding to visit the Science Centre today."

Several streetcars passed, and Vince grew anxious and impatient as he stared along the street.

"At last! O.K., Tom, this next streetcar is yours. Get out at Prince Edward Drive, and ask someone the way to Casa Loma." He made sure Tom was safely on board, then waved good-bye. "I hope you find the diamonds. Save a couple for me!"

Tom walked to a seat at the back of the streetcar as it swayed along the tracks. Only a few passengers were on board; Tom glanced at them, then looked out the window at some kids playing baseball on a school's concrete playground.

Two men in bulky raincoats and floppy hats were waiting at the next stop. The first dropped into a seat at the front as the second struggled into the streetcar on crutches.

The driver offered to help, but the man shook his head and slowly made his way down the aisle. Tom smiled at his choice of both a raincoat and wrap-around sunglasses; the man was obviously prepared for any weather.

Tom shifted closer to the window as the man sat down heavily beside him. Tom wondered briefly why the man hadn't selected an empty seat, then he looked out the window at a push-cart displaying shiny red candy apples and hot cashews. A candy apple would be a perfect reward for finding the diamonds; he wished the streetcar would double its speed.

"Pickpocket! Pickpocket!"

The cry came from the man beside Tom. As the streetcar ground to a halt, the other passengers turned to stare. The man struggled up onto his crutches and pointed an accusing finger at Tom.

"This boy stole my wallet!"

"What?" Tom couldn't believe his ears. "Are you crazy?"

"It's in your pocket!"

Tom looked down, and was stunned to see a worn leather wallet, clearly visible in his pocket. "Hey, what . . . ?"

"You sneaky little thief! Stealing from the handicapped! You should be behind bars."

The other man who'd boarded at the last stop came along the car toward them; close up, the raincoat and hat no longer hid his identity from Tom.

"Hey! You're—"

"Just you be quiet," the man demanded, his strong voice overpowering Tom's. "I'm a police officer, son, and you're under arrest."

"What are you—"

But again Tom was drowned out as the man called for the driver to open the rear doors. He dragged Tom out of the streetcar and toward a van with dark windows. It was parked in an alley. Tom looked round desperately for help, but the alley was deserted. Suddenly he found himself being thrown roughly onto the floor of the van. With a burst of power, it shot off into the traffic of the main street.

Fear pounded through Tom as he looked up from the floor and saw the blacksmith from the stables at Casa Loma leaning menacingly over him.

"Don't move, don't speak," the man said to Tom and then turned toward the driver. "Better slow down. We don't want to be stopped for speeding, especially after I posed as a cop!"

The van slowed down. Tom tried to fight his fear by concentrating on the driver, who he couldn't see from the floor. Who was it? Where were they taking him, and why had he been kidnapped?

As the questions whirled inside Tom's head, he began to panic. He closed his eyes, and tried to think about Liz and the others at Casa Loma; when he didn't return, they'd be sure to call the police.

Time passed, and the van rolled on. Tom's eyes grew heavy, and unwillingly he fell into a troubled sleep.

* * *

He awoke to find the blacksmith shaking his shoulder. "Come with me."

Cold air was blowing in the open door of the van. Tom stumbled out into the black night, and was dragged toward the door of a building. He was bundled down a hallway and shoved into a dark room.

The door closed behind him, and a key turned in the lock.

Light seeped around the locked door, outlining chairs and a sofa; in one corner of the dark room Tom could make out a fireplace.

Low voices came from the hallway on the other side of the door. Tom moved closer, and his stomach tightened in fear as he heard the blacksmith say, "I'll break that kid. He'll tell the truth. It'll take two seconds, or less."

There was a reply from a second voice, probably

that of the driver of the van. Tom strained to hear what was said, but the voice was so low it was barely a murmur.

"Not yet," the blacksmith said. "First, I'm gonna watch the game on TV."

The other voice murmured something.

"I like him," the blacksmith said. "He's got style, with that twenty-four-hour watch and everything. I'm getting one of those when he pays me for this job."

A murmur.

"O.K., so I'm working for *both* of you! Sure, it was you who discovered the study has a latch instead of a button, but you're still not the boss type."

There was the sound of a TV being turned on and suddenly Tom's heart leapt when he heard a voice he knew: Vince Winter.

* * *

Good evening, Vince said. *It's a perfect night for baseball.* As his deep voice went on, describing the baseball game, Tom was filled with an aching loneliness. Would he ever see Liz again, and Uncle Henry?

If only he could escape!

Fantastic! Vince exclaimed. *What a catch by Dexter Valentine!*

The memory of the happy scene on the Valentines' balcony only a few hours before made Tom even more determined to escape. He knew he had to seize the chance provided by the baseball broadcast.

Carefully, he examined the room. There was only the one locked door, and the window had been nailed shut. He was trapped.

Or was he? Tom looked at a small wooden chair in the corner, and considered his chances. Then he went quickly to the chair, picked it up and approached the window.

Using all his strength, Tom swung the chair. With a terrible *crash* the glass broke, showering splinters everywhere. Startled cries came from the hallway as Tom knocked away loose bits of glass and then jumped to the ground.

A light went on inside the room and Tom was caught in its glare. He plunged into the darkness, almost collided with a tree, then stumbled on into the bushes.

"Come back!" the blacksmith shouted.

Tom fought a path through the bushes until he reached the rocky side of a hill. He scrambled on, pausing occasionally to listen for sounds of pursuit. Apart from the cold stars above, he was surrounded by darkness. There was no sound except the shrill calling of frogs, and Tom knew he'd escaped safely.

For a moment this thrilled him, but then a gust of wind chilled his face and he looked around. Where could he possibly go in the endless, empty darkness?

5

For a while Tom blundered on.

He climbed another hill, hoping for signs of civi-
lization, but found only darkness. He thought he heard
traffic, but he was mistaken.

Finally, shivering with cold and fear, Tom sat under
a tree and hugged his body for warmth. It was hopeless
to go further until dawn.

Throughout the long night he dreamed of fireplaces
with roaring flames, and of a luxurious hot bath in
which he was soaking, while diamonds sparkled
nearby. He woke often, his body stiff, then returned to
his dreams.

* * *

Birdsong came before morning. The dawn's faint light revealed a white fungus clinging to a dead stump, then the bare branches of a tree overhead.

At last the sun arrived, and he saw a forest of barren trees, wrapped in mist. Standing, Tom stretched his cramped muscles. If he went toward the sun, which was glowing feebly behind the thick grey mist, he would avoid walking in circles and must eventually find help.

Twigs snapped underfoot as Tom started down the hill. Suddenly he stopped. Was that a car he'd heard? No, it was just the wind gusting through bare branches.

At the foot of the hill, Tom came to a dirt road. A hawk rose from the ditch with something in its talons; briefly it was silhouetted against the cold grey sky before disappearing.

"Wow," Tom whispered. "What a sight."

Hoping that the hawk was a lucky sign, he walked in the direction it had gone. The road was surrounded by the browns and greys of the forest; although it was April, the air was far too cold for the trees to be budding yet.

Despite his stiff muscles, and the hunger which ached inside his stomach, Tom felt cheerful as he followed the road up a hill. People must live around here somewhere, and soon he'd be safe.

At the top of the hill Tom stopped dead in his tracks. Parked on the road ahead was the van used by his kidnappers the previous evening!

Dropping to the ground, Tom studied the van. It was parked near a phone booth, in which Tom could see the blacksmith gesturing with his hand while talking to someone on the phone. The blacksmith hung up and went to speak to a man leaning against the van; with a jolt of surprise, Tom recognized the chauffeur from Casa Loma.

Both men wore red-checked wool coats, and their breath came out in puffs as they nodded agreement at each other. Then they split up, the chauffeur going into the nearby woods while the blacksmith entered the trees on the other side of the road.

When they were lost from sight, Tom hurried toward the phone booth to call the police. He was so cold and tired that he needed help soon, and he was sure the men would take their time searching the woods.

Tom glanced at the back of the van, then reached for the phone. His hand was shaking so much he could hardly hold it.

"Please answer," he whispered, listening as a phone rang in some distant office. "Please!"

As he waited, Tom looked again at the van. Someone was inside, on the driver's side—Tom saw eyes reflected in the rear-view mirror. A ski mask hid the person's face—only the eyes were visible. They darted back and forth across the road, watching the scene.

The ringing stopped, and a voice answered. "Police."

"Uh." Tom stared at the person in the ski mask. He knew those eyes, but where from? "Hello, police?" he whispered.

"Would you speak up? The line's so bad, I can hardly hear you."

"I need help," Tom whispered, slightly louder.

"Please make your call again. I can't hear anything."

"Listen—"

As the line went dead, the eyes spotted Tom. For a moment the person stared in shock, then the van's horn blared. The morning air was shattered by the terrible sound as Tom stumbled out of the booth and started running.

Soon Tom reached the woods—for a second he paused. The horn was still blaring, so the driver must have chosen to signal for the others instead of giving chase. This was a real break, and Tom used it to plunge deeper into the trees.

At last the horn stopped. Tom reached a stony outcrop and looked down into a deep river, swollen with the spring flood. Crawling behind a rock, he tried desperately to think. How could he save himself?

A minute later, Tom had a plan. Putting his shoulder against the largest boulder on the outcropping, he worked it loose. Then he waited until he could hear the sound of feet crashing through the trees.

Tom pushed with all his strength against the boulder. It hesitated, then rolled over the edge of the outcropping, and plunged down toward the swirling black water below. As it fell, Tom cupped his mouth and screamed, "No!"

The boulder hit the water with a tremendous splash. Tom scrambled along the outcropping to the shelter of a big tree and dropped behind it, shaking with fear.

"That was the kid," the blacksmith shouted from somewhere in the trees. "He must have fallen in the river!"

"Perfect," cried the chauffeur. "Let's go fish him out."

The chattering of an angry squirrel announced the approach of the men. Tom held his breath.

"Look at that water," the blacksmith exclaimed. "He didn't have a chance. I can't even see his body."

"We'd better get outta here."

They hurried away, but Tom remained in hiding long after he'd heard the van drive off. It was possible the men suspected a trick, and one had remained behind to watch the woods.

Finally hunger and cold forced Tom to move. He worked his way cautiously back toward the road until he could see the phone booth. There was no sign of the men. He hurried to the phone booth, desperate now to contact the police. But the phone was dead.

"They've cut the line! I don't believe it."

Tom stared at the useless instrument, feeling his spirits ebb away. What should he do now? Slumped against the booth, Tom stared at the grey mist and barren trees.

The men might return at any moment. Tom knew he must move on, yet he couldn't find the energy; it didn't seem.worth the effort. Then, to his surprise, a porcupine came out of the woods and lumbered slowly across the road. Tom looked at its sharp quills, smiling at the porcupine's rolling gait. It looked like a nearsighted gentleman, bound for the Millionaires' Club.

One more try. Tom started along the road on feet that felt like blocks of ice, blowing on his pinched fingers for warmth. A tiny bird swept out of a pine tree and swooped round Tom's head, defending its nest. Tom trudged wearily on.

Then Tom saw a lake. In the distance, along the

shoreline, there was a large cabin with a twist of smoke rising from its stone chimney.

"People! At last, real people! I'm saved!"

At this moment, as if in a final effort to break his spirit, rain began to fall. Big drops splattered on Tom's face as he left the road to follow the shoreline to the distant cabin.

"Don't be a mirage," he begged. "Please stay where you are."

A flock of small birds explored the wild grass along the shoreline. A blue heron took off from the shore, rising gracefully over the still lake where raindrops were forming hundreds of perfect circles.

Reaching the cabin, Tom noticed a ribbon of road winding out of the woods to a garage with a moss-covered roof. Both doors of the garage were closed. The road was littered with dead branches from winter storms, giving it a deserted appearance, but recent tire tracks and fresh footsteps leading from the garage to the cabin suggested that the cabin was in active use. Beside the footsteps in the wet ground were two long, thin tracks.

Tom thumped on the cabin's side door with his hand, and called for help. When there was no reply, he hit the door again, feeling his numb hand throb with pain.

"Who's there?" a voice shouted from inside.

The thrill of hearing the voice, and knowing he was truly safe, fed energy into Tom's system. "Help me," he cried.

"Be right with you."

Tom stepped back from the door, blowing on his

cold hands. Moving about to keep his blood circulating, he went around to the front of the cabin.

One of the windows was smashed.

Tom stared at the scattered glass, refusing to believe his eyes. Then he heard the cabin door open, and his heart jumped as he turned to see the blacksmith.

6

The man glared at Tom.

"So you tricked us, boy."

"No," Tom whispered. "Please, leave me alone."

The blacksmith walked forward, his huge hands clenched. Tom stared past him at the woods, realizing he couldn't reach their safety, then he ran toward the lake.

A pier stood over the water. Tom's feet slipped on the pier's wet surface as he ran to the end. There were no boats. He looked at the rain falling on the black water. Knowing it was foolish to even consider swimming across the cold lake, he turned to face the blacksmith. The pier was narrow, and there was no hope of darting past the man to safety.

"Get away from me," Tom begged, backing away.

He took another step back, but his foot found only emptiness. With a cry he fell backwards into the lake! Freezing water closed over his head, then Tom struggled to the surface and swam toward the pier. With the last of his energy he climbed a ladder from the water, and collapsed at the blacksmith's feet.

The man lifted Tom in his powerful arms. "Enjoy your swim?"

"Leave me alone," Tom gasped. "I'm . . . I'm . . ."

"Where are the diamonds?"

Tom stared at him.

"Tell me where the diamonds are hidden," the man demanded.

"I . . ." Tom could hardly control his chattering teeth. "I . . . don't . . . know."

The blacksmith stepped toward the water. "In you go."

"No! I'll tell."

"You've got two seconds, then you're back in the lake."

"They're . . ." Tom gasped for breath. "They're in . . . Sir Nigel's . . . shower."

The blacksmith's piggy eyes studied Tom's face, and for a terrible moment the man seemed ready to throw him into the lake again. Then he nodded.

"I think you're telling the truth."

"I . . . am!"

"For your sake, I hope so."

Carrying Tom in his powerful arms, the blacksmith returned to the cabin. Soon Tom was lying in a hot bath, feeling it draw the chill from his bones.

Later he sat at a rough-cut wooden table, watching the blacksmith throw chunks of log into a potbellied stove. Despite what had happened, Tom was too hungry to feel anything but thankful as the man dropped bacon, and then eggs, into a sizzling frying pan.

Tom's clothes were drying beside the stove. The blacksmith had provided an old dressing-gown; Tom pulled it tighter around himself.

"Where's the chauffeur?"

No reply.

"And the driver of the van. You know who I mean. I don't see them around."

The blacksmith scooped the bacon and eggs onto a tin plate, and dropped it in front of Tom on the table. He looked at Tom without speaking, then returned to the stove.

The first taste of food was marvellous. "This is great! May I have some toast, please?" Tom swallowed quickly, loving the crispy bacon and the superb eggs. "You three will be arrested for kidnapping. Doesn't that worry you?"

The blacksmith poured coffee from a blackened pot, then downed the hot beverage in one long swallow. He hadn't spoken a word since leaving the pier.

"You're a terrific cook," Tom said, trying to get the silent man talking. "You should be a chef, not a criminal. You don't seem the outlaw type to me."

The blacksmith glanced at Tom, and something flickered in his eyes. "It's time for you to get some sleep," he said gruffly. "I'm tired of your questions."

Tom fell silent, afraid he had pushed the man too far. He was led to a room with a bare mattress and a sleeping bag. Crawling into it, he burrowed a warm place and closed his eyes. With vivid clarity, Tom re-enacted in his mind the scene as he had approached the cabin. He recalled the rising smoke and the dead branches on the road, but he was sure the memory held something else that was really important. He'd almost figured it out when he fell asleep.

Some time later, the blacksmith shook him awake. Barely able to focus his eyes, Tom dragged on his clothes and was taken outside, where the van was waiting. Someone wearing a ski mask sat at the wheel.

Tom dropped into the rear seat and wearily closed his eyes. Then suddenly, without warning, he was blindfolded and shoved onto the floor by the blacksmith.

"Oh no! Hey, it's horrible down here. Please let me up."

His pleas were in vain. The van was soon under way, and Tom remained on the floor. Again he slept, but fitfully.

* * *

Tom was awakened by the squeal of brakes. Rough hands seized him, and he was pushed out of the van. Tearing off his blindfold, Tom tried to get the licence plate number but he was unsuccessful. He watched the vehicle disappear from the small park in which Tom had been abandoned.

Delighted to be free, Tom looked around the park. There was no sign of people, so he hurried toward the sound of traffic to find help.

By the time he reached the street, he'd had time to think. It would be better if he found the diamonds before contacting the police. He stopped a woman and asked her where he could catch a streetcar to Casa Loma.

She pointed at a TTC sign. "Take the subway to the Dupont stop."

"Thanks."

It was a long ride and Tom tried to curb his impatience by sitting in the front car, where he watched signal lights flash past as the train raced through twisting tunnels beneath Toronto. At Dupont he climbed to the street and hurried toward Casa Loma; in just a few more minutes he could tell Uncle Henry about the shower and help him to take it apart. He just hoped that the crooks hadn't got there first.

Tom rushed from room to room until he spotted Liz and his uncle in the conservatory.

Swinging open a door, he hurried in. "I'm back!"

Liz glanced his way. "Hi, Tom."

Uncle Henry smiled. "Enjoy your swim? I hope the water wasn't too cold."

Staggered, Tom stared at the two. Surely they weren't involved in his kidnapping? His shock then turned to amazement as they returned to their conversation.

"Hey," he cried aloud. "I'm safe!"

Liz looked his way, puzzled. "Have you been nibbling mouldy crackers again? Of course you're safe."

"Well, don't you care?"

"You're spoiling our fun, Tom. We're trying to act nonchalant, so you won't know we've got a secret."

"But don't you realize I was *kidnapped* yesterday?"

"Sure you were," Liz said. "And the cow jumped over the moon."

"Listen to me! I was grabbed by the Casa Loma

blacksmith and chauffeur, taken to some cabin, chased through the woods, I don't know what all happened. Then I come home to *this*! Where do you think I've been all this time?"

Uncle Henry polished his glasses thoughtfully. "The chauffeur's wife phoned last night, Tom. She said you'd be staying overnight. You were delighted because their apartment building has a swimming pool."

"Lies!"

"So I gather." Uncle Henry looked concerned. "What actually happened?"

Tom told the full story, including his theory about the diamonds' hiding-place. Liz and Uncle Henry glanced at each other when he mentioned the jewels, but remained silent.

Uncle Henry polished his glasses again. "This is serious, Tom. We must contact the police."

"What's the use? Both men will be in hiding by now. Besides, I've got no proof against them, and I haven't clue one where that cabin is located."

"What about the third person?"

"I could only see the driver's eyes. I couldn't make an ID. Hey, I'm starving. Do you think Irene would fetch me a snack?"

"Irene's left us."

"Irene? I don't believe it!"

Uncle Henry shook his head unhappily. "I'm afraid it's true. According to the other servants, Irene suddenly announced she was quitting. She walked out and didn't say good-bye."

"What a rotten thing to do."

Uncle Henry sighed. "I don't understand. After she's been so friendly."

"Do you think she quit because of Smythe?"

"Who knows? Anyway, we've seen the last of Smythe. He's quit too."

"*What!*"

Uncle Henry tried to smile. "It seems I'm not a very successful employer. The staff of Casa Loma is in tatters, and I've only been here three days."

"Surely no one else has gone?"

"A couple of others resigned, and Tia had to go home yesterday. She's got the flu. I can't get replacements until she's back, and can interview the candidates."

His face was so bleak that Tom almost smiled. Running a castle wasn't proving to be much fun; any more staff losses and Uncle Henry's entire day would be spent cleaning the fifteen bathrooms and replacing Casa Loma's five thousand light bulbs.

"Cheer up, Unc. Let's check Sir Nigel's shower for the diamonds."

"I almost forgot!" Uncle Henry smiled at Liz. "We haven't told Tom our secret."

They led Tom down Peacock Alley to the door of Sir Nigel's study. Uncle Henry unlocked it, waved the others inside, then secured the door against intruders.

Puzzled, Tom looked at the oil paintings of ancient gentlemen in wigs, then at the chandelier and the mahogany walls. He wondered what the big secret could be. Liz went to stand by the marble fireplace, while Uncle Henry sat at the desk and ran his fingers over one of its carved eagles.

"Look at this, Tom." Uncle Henry opened a drawer.

He slid aside a secret panel, then took a small velvet box from hiding.

Tom shivered with excitement as the box was put in his hands. He lifted the top, and his eyes were dazzled by the white fire inside.

"The diamonds! I don't believe it!"

7

For a few minutes, Tom could only stare.

"But . . . ? How . . . ?"

"It was simple." Uncle Henry put his feet on the desk, and fiddled happily with an old quill pen. "Want to know how we found them?"

"Of course!"

"Well, we just opened the secret drawer." He smiled. "Of course, we had a little help before that."

"What help?"

"Someone phoned this morning, Tom. He wouldn't give his name, but he explained exactly where to find the diamonds. Vince Winter was here having coffee, so the two of us plus Liz and Smythe dashed to the study . . . and you know the rest."

"Brother! After all my running around in the woods,

and a ducking in the lake, I finally get set to dig out the diamonds and you've beaten me to it!"

"Sorry, Tom. Maybe we should have waited for you."

Tom tried to smile. "I'm glad you found the diamonds. Too bad Sir Nigel wasn't in the desk too."

"I agree. He could have his crazy castle back." Uncle Henry looked at his watch. "I'd better go and arrange for afternoon tea. The cook may forget, now there isn't a butler to keep things happening on time."

When he'd left, Liz smiled. "We were in the kitchen this morning. The stove is actually big enough to roast a whole ox."

"Is that right, eh?"

"You sound blue, Tom."

"Yeah." He put his finger in the velvet box, and pushed around the glittering jewels. "Shouldn't these be somewhere safe?"

"Uncle Henry is leaving them hidden in the desk overnight. Tomorrow they're going into a safety-deposit box at the bank."

"Will they be O.K. here?"

"Sure. The rest of the servants will probably soon resign, so there'll be no one to steal them."

Tom watched Liz put away the velvet box, then close the secret panel.

"There's still a lot of unanswered questions, Liz. For example, the clue Sir Nigel gave Tia doesn't fit with a desk drawer, although I suppose he could have been just teasing." Tom walked over to the marble fireplace. "There's also that weird thing I overheard the blacksmith say. When I was being held prisoner at the cabin."

"What was that?"

"Something about the study having a latch instead of a button. I thought maybe he was talking about this study, since this is where Sir Nigel disappeared."

"Well, it beats me." Liz commented.

Still chilly from his night in the open, Tom decided to take a shower. Leaving Liz sitting in the study, staring at a scrap of paper on which she'd written *study-latch-button*, he went off to Sir Nigel's private suite to use the fancy shower.

To his delight, it decided to co-operate this time, and thin needles of hot water hissed from the rails until Tom had nearly drained the castle's boiler. Lazily he dried himself. He was sorry he hadn't been correct about the shower concealing the diamonds, but he was glad they were safe.

Returning to the study, he found Liz with her feet on the desk and a wrap-around grin on her face.

"I deserve a large medal," she said.

"What happened?"

"Tell me again about Irene opening the secret panel in Sir Nigel's bedroom?"

"Well, she just pushed a button under the mantel, and the panel swung open."

"Don't you get it? In the bedroom a button, in the study . . ."

"A latch!"

"Watch this." Liz crossed the luxurious rug and reached under the wooden mantel above the fireplace.

Silently, a mahogany panel swung open in the wall.

"Good grief!" Tom went forward to gaze at the narrow stairs leading down into darkness. "Well done, Liz."

"Thanks," she said, smiling.

"Where do they go?"

"Don't ask me. I'm too chicken to go down there alone."

Gingerly, Tom put his foot on the top stair. It creaked, and he stepped quickly back.

"Come on," Liz said. "Let's try them together."

Tom followed her into the darkness. The narrow wooden stairs spiralled down, and soon the light of the study was left behind. The air was musty and freezing cold.

"Concrete," Liz whispered. "I think we've reached a tunnel."

"There must be a light." Tom stretched out his hand, and his fingers touched cold cement. He felt his way along it, but found no light switches.

"Want to turn back?" Liz whispered.

"No way. Let's see where this leads."

Liz's face was a dim white smudge in the darkness. She started along the tunnel, then disappeared.

"Slow down," Tom said. "I can't see anything."

"Keep your hand on the wall as a guide."

"What if there's an open pit ahead? Filled with alligators."

"Nice thing to say, when I'm going first."

They both fell silent. The only sound came from their hesitant footsteps and nervous breathing as, slowly and carefully, Tom and Liz worked their way forward through the cold black air.

"This is crazy," Tom whispered after a while. "We could walk forever."

"The tunnel must lead somewhere."

"Two more minutes, then we turn back."

"O.K."

Tom's nerves were on edge as he pictured water-filled pits and spiders with fangs waiting in the darkness. He was beginning to wish the secret panel had remained a secret when an urgent *hssst!* came from Liz.

"Stairs," she whispered. "Leading up."

The wooden stairs creaked underfoot. At the top Liz searched the wall for an opening. Suddenly there was a *click*, and pale light seeped through a narrow crack.

"We're in the stables!"

"Are you sure?"

The crack grew wider as Liz pushed open a panel in the wall. Tom could see the narrow passage that led to the horse stalls.

"So! This is how they got Sir Nigel and Hatfield out of the study."

Liz nodded. "The blacksmith probably did the dirty work. He must have knocked Sir Nigel over the head, then hauled him through the tunnel to the stables. Ditto with Hatfield."

"But then what happened?"

"Listen!" The urgency in his sister's voice made Tom's hair stand up.

From somewhere in the stables came a muffled thudding. Tom grew tense as he followed Liz along the passage toward the sound; what if the blacksmith was waiting with one of his mallets?

Turning a corner, they found themselves at the horse stalls. The thudding was much louder.

"It's coming from that end stall," Liz said.

They hurried across the tiled floor to the stall's pad-locked door. Tom found a pair of the blacksmith's tongs, and used them to force the padlock off.

Liz gave the door a quick shove, and with a squeal of metal, it swung open to reveal a small cot.

Lying on the cot was Sir Nigel Brampton.

His face was flushed from the effort of kicking the wall, and his eyes goggled as he tried to speak through the gag over his mouth. "*Mmmmmph!*" he said, gestur-ing with his bound hands.

"It's O.K.," Tom replied. "We'll get you untied."

As Tom bent over the knots, Sir Nigel continued to make anxious sounds. The moment Liz removed his gag, Sir Nigel burst out, "The diamonds! Are they safe?"

"They sure are." Liz smiled. "And now you're safe, too."

"The jewels . . . are you positive?"

"We've just been looking at them. Now try to relax, Sir Nigel. Tom's almost got those knots undone."

"Thank goodness my diamonds are safe. Those crooks tried everything to make me reveal the hiding-place, but I refused!"

"That's great."

As Tom released the final knot, Sir Nigel sat up on the cot. He smoothed the white hair which fringed his bald head, then smiled. "Thank you for rescuing me. I've kicked and kicked that wall, but no one ever heard." He tried to stand, then sank back with a groan.

"You're not well," Liz said anxiously. "We'd better get help."

"Nonsense. I'm fine." Sir Nigel staggered up, but again he collapsed. "Perhaps you're right. I do need assistance."

Tom went to the door. "Wait here. I'll ask Uncle Henry to phone for an ambulance." Hurrying through the stables, he noticed the forge and suddenly realized why the blacksmith was always pounding cold horse-shoes. Obviously it was to drown out Sir Nigel's efforts to attract attention when anyone came to the stables.

A second puzzle was answered when Tom remembered the chauffeur with the tray of food. He must have brought it through the tunnel for Sir Nigel, which explained his dry clothes.

The jigsaw was slowly falling together, and yet Tom didn't feel elated. Somehow, he sensed the mystery and danger were far from over.

8

The big man swung hard.

There was a loud *crack* as bat and ball connected.
Dexter Valentine dove for the ball, then threw it with
lightning speed to first base.

"You're out!" the umpire shouted, as the batter
reached the base a split-second after the ball.

Thousands of cheering voices filled the night, and
another Blue Jays baseball game was under way.

"Did you see that play?" Tom exclaimed. "That was
my buddy, Dexter!"

Liz laughed. "Your buddy? You didn't know the
guy two days ago."

"I make friends fast." Tom turned to look at Vince
Winter inside a nearby glass-walled broadcast booth.
Vince could be seen describing Dexter's sensational

play; although the booth was sound-proofed, it was clear that Vince's words were filled with awe at the player's skill.

A cold wind came off nearby Lake Ontario, slicing through Tom's clothes. He shivered, and looked longingly at a man who was carrying a steaming container through the crowd. "Hot dogs," the man cried. "Get your giant red-hots here!"

"You hungry, Liz?"

She nodded. "I'm going for a Salty Pretzel. Can I get you a hot cat?"

"You bet!"

Tom leaned against the railing which separated the broadcast area from the crowd, and returned to watching the action on the stadium's ultra-green artificial turf.

Dexter was first up for the Blue Jays. He let two strikes past, then sent the ball flashing into left field for a clean single. As the crowd erupted in cheers, Liz returned with the food. "Why the thanksgiving? Is the game over?"

"Funny, funny. Dexter just happens to be a hero, yet again."

"I'm frozen solid." Leaning over the railing, Liz pointed at a man whose head was hidden inside a tuque that read *Go Jays Go*. "I'd love one of those tuques. It would be a great souvenir of Toronto."

The next pitch was fouled off into the crowd. There was generous applause for the girl who proudly held up the ball after a mad scramble among the fans.

"That's the souvenir I'd like," Tom said. "Or even a broken bat."

Seconds later, as the pitcher unleashed a knuckle-ball, Dexter broke for second base. The crowd rose, screaming, as the throw to second seemed to have Dexter trapped, but with a burst of speed he slid to safety under the tag. The cheering continued as he brushed dirt off his uniform, then grinned.

"Fantastic," Liz said. "Your buddy puts on a great show."

"I predict he'll score the first run."

On the next pitch, the batter rattled a double off the wall, and Dexter crossed home plate to put Toronto in the lead.

The Milwaukee pitcher was in deep trouble, and Tom felt sorry for the man as the team's manager walked slowly to the mound, frowning. They spoke briefly, then the unhappy pitcher handed over the ball and started toward the dugout.

"He's heading for the showers. Maybe he'll get lucky and find some diamonds there!"

On the stadium's huge screen, the pitcher was seen trudging woefully across the field. As this image froze and was replaced by a junk-food commercial, Tom remembered Sir Nigel's clue to Tia about where he'd hidden the diamonds. The clue couldn't possibly have referred to the desk drawer, and again Tom felt uneasy.

"Why am I nervous about the diamonds?"

"Because it was all so simple. One anonymous phone call, and suddenly the mystery is solved." Liz looked thoughtfully at the cold darkness beyond the stadium, where a winking neon sign advertised a TV station. "Something about the discovery of the diamonds smells like a very old egg."

The new Milwaukee pitcher quickly got his team out of trouble, and Toronto clung to its one-run lead as the fast-paced action continued. During the seventh-inning stretch, Vince joined Tom and Liz. "I've brought some binoculars, if you'd care to try them."

Tom smiled at the sportscaster. "Can't you arrange for Dexter to foul one up here, so we'll have a souvenir?"

"Although I've worked many miracles, Tom, that one could be difficult. However, I do believe you'll be leaving with a souvenir."

"Wow! What is it?"

"Patience, patience."

Using the binoculars, Liz studied the people huddled under blankets and shaggy coats. "You know something?" she said at last. "I'm sure that's Smythe the butler down there."

Vince grabbed the binoculars. "Let me look!"

Vince carefully studied the man Liz pointed out. Then he smiled. "You're wrong, Liz. His nose is a different shape."

"What about that hacked-up chin?"

"Some other guy with a dull razor blade. Not everyone is wise enough to buy the electric shavers I advertise on TV."

Liz tried again with the binoculars. "That *is* Smythe. I noticed him a while ago, because he kept looking up here. I wonder what's going on?"

Vince laughed. "The only action is in your imagination, Liz."

Vince returned to the booth and Tom tried the binoculars, but saw only the man's back as he hurried toward an exit. "Why would Smythe be here? I remember him saying only kooks like pro sports."

With a roar, the crowd rose to its feet. A Blue Jays slugger had connected solidly, and the ball was high in the air, gleaming against the black sky. Tracing an arc through the night, it landed beyond the wall for a home run.

"I don't believe it!" Tom released a war whoop, and pounded his hands together. "What a hit!"

The Blue Jays left the dugout to congratulate their latest hero, and the crowd applauded for several minutes. Then they settled back anxiously, wondering if Milwaukee would stage a comeback.

By the time the game was over, Tom's fingernails were a mess and the Blue Jays had a 2–0 win. After studying the remains of the money he'd saved for his holiday, Tom decided he could afford hot dogs for Liz and himself.

As they ate, Vince joined them. "You two interested in meeting the Blue Jays? I'm just about to do some interviews."

"For sure!"

Deep inside the stadium, happy talk and laughter came from the Blue Jays' dressing-room. In a separate room, a TV camera was set up for Vince's interviews with some players.

The last to be interviewed was Dexter Valentine, and afterwards Tom proudly introduced him to Liz. Vince then handed Dexter a large carton. He whispered something to the baseball player, who then smiled at Tom and Liz.

"Liz and Tom," Dexter said, sounding rather self-conscious and strained, "I understand you rescued Sir Nigel today?"

"Sort of, I guess," Liz replied. "We just looked in the right place."

"I've been asked to present you both with a souvenir, to mark his rescue."

"Thanks!"

Tom and Liz grinned at Dexter and then thanked Vince, who waved his hand. "You deserve it, kids."

Dexter opened the carton to reveal two satin team-jackets with thick crests reading *Toronto Blue Jays*, and baseball caps with crests. Tom and Liz were delighted, and immediately put them on.

"You look good," Vince said. "Let me get a picture of you with Dexter."

The camera flashed, then Dexter said good-bye. Vince smiled at Tom and Liz. "Feel like a day at Niagara Falls? I'm going there to interview a retired tennis pro. Would your uncle let you go as my guests?"

"He'd better!"

"Then let's drive up to the castle. You can collect your toothbrushes, and we'll leave tonight. That way we'll get an early start on the sights of Niagara Falls."

Uncle Henry gave permission for the journey, but seemed depressed about something. They left him slumped in front of the fireplace waiting for Sir Nigel, who had insisted on being discharged from hospital and was expected at any minute.

"I wonder what's wrong?" Tom said, as they walked towards Vince's sports car. "Do you think Uncle Henry is feeling blue because he won't be taking over the castle?"

Liz shook her head. "No, something else is bothering Unc."

"Maybe it's the diamonds. I still say there's something weird about how you found them so easily."

9

Rocking and bucking, the little boat headed toward the Horseshoe Falls.

From high above, emerald-green water plunged down with great force, forming a steaming white spray.

"This is fantastic!" Tom had to shout above the thundering roar of the falls.

Liz laughed as her face was lashed by needles of spray. "I'm drowning!"

Wrapped in rain-slickers, they stood with Vince in the bow of the *Maid of the Mist* as it fought the seething green water. Tom could now see nothing except the white spray which stung his face until he was blinded. He was worried that the captain had taken them too far in and the boat would be crushed to pieces by the terrible fury of the falls. For many years, tourists have ventured deep into the heart of the falls in these brave little boats.

The captain put the boat into reverse and the *Maid of the Mist* slipped slowly out of the spray. Licking water off his lips, Tom grinned.

Vince pulled back the hood of his slicker, and shook water out of his wavy brown hair. Then he pointed up to the top of the falls, where a crowd of people were watching the *Maid of the Mist* from a high cliff. "That's called Table Rock House. From there, elevators take tourists deep inside the rock to tunnels which lead to openings behind the falls. Let's go take a look."

"Is it safe?" Tom asked.

"Let's hope so!"

The boat swung around, and started toward its dock. Tom watched gulls dipping and soaring in the air currents caused by the cascading falls. A fine mist drifted over the gorge's green waters, and the air smelled wonderfully fresh.

"What a day! The best of my life."

Vince smiled. "The excitement isn't over yet."

After they'd docked, and returned the rain-slickers, Vince and Liz paused at mirrors provided by the company to comb their damp hair. Tom ran a quick hand through his hair, then put on the Blue Jays cap and adjusted his team-jacket, anxious to start the next part of the adventure.

They took an elevator to the top of the gorge where Vince had left his sports car. "There's Rainbow Bridge," he said, pointing. "It crosses to the American side of the falls."

"You mean that's the USA, just across the gorge?"

Vince nodded. "We'll cross the bridge and look at the falls from the American viewpoint after we've seen those tunnels."

"*If* we survive the tunnels," Tom said, attempting a laugh.

* * *

A short while later, they were walking toward Table Rock House when Liz suddenly pointed at a newspaper box. "Hey, look at that headline!"

Under a photograph of Sir Nigel, a huge black headline read: BORDER ALERT FOR GEMS. Inserting a coin in the box, Liz seized a paper and quickly scanned the article.

"That explains everything!"

"What's it say, Liz?"

She looked up from the newspaper, her eyes shining with excitement. "Those so-called diamonds we found at Casa Loma were fakes! They were cheap imitations made from quartz. The police figure the real diamonds have been taken from the castle."

"Why the border alert?" Vince asked.

"Apparently the police think a couple of Americans are the masterminds behind the theft, and may be heading for the USA with the diamonds. Travellers are being questioned at border checkpoints, and some people are being searched."

"What a great story!" Vince looked envious as he read the article. "Sometimes I'd love to be in TV news, not sports. Then for sure I'd dig up lots of hot news items like this. I could become an anchor on network TV."

Tom began reading the story. "Thank goodness Sir Nigel came home last night, and discovered the truth about the diamonds."

Liz shook her head. "Keep reading, Tom. The police knew the diamonds were fakes long before Sir Nigel got home."

"But how did they know that?"

No one could suggest an answer. Tom turned to the sports page, hoping to find the photograph Vince had taken of them with Dexter Valentine, but the only picture showed Dexter making a sensational diving catch. Under the photograph, a caption read: *Dexter Valentine—America's greatest player of all time!*

Vince looked at his watch. "Come on, people."

Outside the entrance to Table Rock House, they paused to gaze down into the gorge. Far below, the *Maid of the Mist* was just disappearing into the white spray; Tom shivered with excitement as he looked at the massive weight of green water plunging down.

"Imagine going over those falls. You'd be knocked to pieces."

Vince nodded. "A lot of people have died here. But a few survived."

"Went over the falls and lived? Impossible!"

Vince pointed at the wide river which rushed through a series of rapids before dropping over the falls. "Back in 1901, a widowed teacher was set adrift on the river inside an oak barrel. She was looking for instant fame and fortune by being the first to survive the plunge."

"Did she live?" Liz asked.

"Yes, but the only money she made was from selling autographed pictures of herself beside the barrel.

She died a pauper. Then some guy went over safely in a barrel, only to die later after slipping on a piece of orange peel."

Tom stared at the roaring water, finding it hard to believe that such strange events had happened right here. "I think Mr. Stones told our class about some kid surviving the falls."

Vince nodded. "A seven-year-old boy was in a boating accident on the river. His life-jacket kept him afloat all through the rapids, and he was so light that he was then thrown straight out over the falls. He landed beyond the rocks, and was picked up by the *Maid of the Mist*. No damage done, except a couple of cuts."

Liz looked at a log trapped between two boulders near the lip of the falls, then stared at the foaming white rapids. "Imagine boating on such a dangerous river. If I ever do that, please have my head tested."

Vince laughed. "You're right, Liz. Although I'm an avid sportsman, a boat ride through the Niagara rapids is one thrill I'm not after."

"Speaking of thrills, how about those tunnels?"

"Follow me!"

Inside Table Rock House, they were directed to a changing-room which looked like a scene from a science fiction movie. Attendants dressed in yellow prepared the tourists for the tunnels by replacing their shoes with huge gumboots and wrapping each person inside a black rubber rain-slicker and hood. At Vince's suggestion, Tom and Liz kept their Blue Jays caps and team-jackets on under their slickers. "Those outfits are valuable," Vince said, smiling.

Tom waddled toward the elevator, his feet sliding around inside the gumboots. His head was buried beneath the greasy rubber hood. Smiling, he watched a large group of tourists chattering happily in a foreign language as they posed for pictures in their black gear.

Then everyone jammed inside the elevator for the trip down. The noisy conversation continued until the elevator doors opened without warning and the tourists were silenced by the roar of the falls.

The booming thunder of the water filled the narrow tunnel. A little child belonging to one of the tourists started to cry. He was picked up as the group shuffled out of the elevator.

"This way," Vince yelled, pointing along the tunnel.

Tom nodded and smiled, but his heart was beating fast. The deafening noise of the water made him wonder if they should keep away from the plunging falls. But then he realized that it must be safe, or tourists would not be allowed down here.

"Fabulous, eh?" he shouted to Liz.

She smiled nervously. "I hope Vince knows what he's doing! I'd hate to fall in."

"We'll be fine!"

The long tunnel was lined with orange, white and red lights. Tom was again reminded of a scene from a science fiction movie as he looked at the eerie figures of the other tourists, hidden inside their identical black slickers. A person could commit a murder here, and never be identified.

Rounding a corner, he suddenly saw the water.

It fell in a solid sheet of white, roaring down to the rocks and steaming up in clouds of spray through the narrow tunnel opening. Tom stared at it in fascination.

Finally he backed away, and followed a second tunnel toward another opening. There were yet more tourists here, and he had to wait his turn to approach the flimsy wooden railing which warned *Danger: do not climb over*.

At that moment, a man at the railing turned his head.

It was Smythe.

10

The Casa Loma butler returned to studying the plunging water, and was again camouflaged by his hooded slicker. Tom's heart thumped fearfully, and he moved carefully away, hoping he wouldn't be spotted.

Tom hurried to the other tunnel. "Vince," he shouted, going from figure to figure until he found him. "I just saw Smythe!"

Vince looked stunned. "Are you certain?"

"Yes! It was him, shaving cuts and all. He's in the other tunnel!"

Vince was silent for a moment. Then he led Tom and Liz away from the other tourists. "Listen carefully," he said. "It's time for the truth. I'm a Mountie, working undercover on the Casa Loma case. Things are getting hot. I'll need your help or the crooks might get away!"

"Wow," Tom exclaimed. "Sure thing!"

"The real reason I'm at Niagara Falls is to watch for Smythe, in case he tries to cross the border with the diamonds. Thanks to your quick eyes, Tom, he's been spotted."

Tom glowed. Liz patted his back.

"I can't tackle him alone, in case he's armed and someone gets shot." Vince quickly outlined a plan, then Tom rushed back to the tunnel where he'd spotted Smythe.

It was jammed with tourists, and Tom's spirits sank as he hurried from figure to figure without finding Smythe. Had the suspect made a getaway? Then suddenly Tom spotted the man.

"Smythe! Please help me!"

Looking shocked, the man stared at Tom.

"Quick," Tom cried. "My sister's in terrible danger!"

Tom started to run. He glanced over his shoulder at Smythe close behind, then pushed through the tourists toward the thundering water where Liz stood waiting.

She turned, her face wet with spray, and screamed when she saw Smythe. Her legs buckled, and she collapsed to the rocky ground beside the thundering falls.

"Help her!" Tom cried.

Smythe pushed Tom aside, and bent over Liz. Just then Vince came along the tunnel with two muscular-looking men in slickers. "That's him," he yelled, pointing at Smythe. "You see, he's tried to push that girl over the side. Grab him!"

Smythe glanced up, puzzled, then gave a startled cry as the men seized his arms and shoved him against the rock wall. Liz scrambled to her feet, and quickly followed Tom along the tunnel. Behind them, Smythe shouted something but his words were lost in the roar of the water.

Vince joined them at the elevator, his eyes bright. "Good work! Those men will hold Smythe until we return with police help."

The elevator doors closed on the fury of the water. The silence was a sudden contrast to the noise which had been pounding inside Tom's head. Releasing a deep sigh, he looked at Vince.

"Who's your second suspect?"

"What?"

"The newspaper said two Americans are behind the theft."

"Oh." Vince paused to shake water out of his hair. "I'm sorry, but I can't give you that information."

"Is it someone I know?"

Vince smiled. "O.K., I admit you know the person."

"Then . . ."

Vince raised a hand. "No more questions."

Tom tapped his foot impatiently as the elevator rose slowly inside the cliff. "Is it a man or a woman?" he asked Vince.

At that moment the elevator reached the top. Soon they were running across the crowded parking lot to Vince's car. He pulled out of the parking lot at top speed and headed through the crowded streets of the tourist town.

"Where's the police station?" Tom shouted, hanging on tight as they flew around a corner.

"Not far."

Liz looked at Vince. "Isn't that the Rainbow Bridge straight ahead?"

Vince nodded. "We're crossing to the American side to alert the FBI to increase their border guard. Smythe's partner is almost certainly here too."

Reaching the middle of the bridge, they passed the flags of Canada, the United Nations and the USA. Tom looked beyond the flags to the distant Horseshoe Falls, then straight down at the swirling waters of the gorge far below.

"Hopping horntoads! That's a long drop."

Vince laughed. "How'd you like to cross this gorge on a tightrope?"

"No thanks! Not for every diamond in the world."

"The Great Blondin did a lot of tightrope stunts over this gorge." Slowing down on the bridge, they joined a line of vehicles waiting to pass through the border checkpoint. "The Great Blondin did back-somersaults, rode a bike across, even cooked an omelette out there."

"Cheese or mushroom?" Liz asked.

Vince laughed, then gestured impatiently. "What a time to be delayed! Come on, traffic, move!"

"Put on your siren, and pass the others," Tom suggested.

"This sports car didn't come with a siren." Vince chewed a fingernail, then relaxed as they moved closer to the checkpoint. "It's O.K., kids! We're going to make it safely."

"Did the Great Blob ever fall?" Liz asked.

"Nope. But he came close, when he carried a man across on his back and the tightrope swayed wildly. But they managed to reach safety."

Liz shook her head. "Men are crazy."

"A woman did stunts, too. She walked the tightrope backwards, then crossed with her head covered by a bag. Another time she had her feet inside peach baskets."

"What a way to make a buck!"

"You're right, Liz." Vince smiled happily. "I'm making lots of bucks, but not by risking my neck."

They drove toward a row of booths where multi-coloured flags flapped in the wind and uniformed officials questioned occupants of the vehicles coming off the bridge.

"I'll do the talking," Vince said, stopping the car at a booth. Getting out, he had a short conversation with the official, but only his charming laugh could be heard from inside the car.

"This is no laughing matter," Liz said. "Smythe could have escaped by now."

"Not with those two big bruisers holding him. But I still wish Vince would hurry!"

Finally Vince got back into the car, and drove to a nearby parking lot. "They need me inside the customs office. I won't be long. You kids, stay here."

"Have the officials seen anything of Smythe's partner?"

"Apparently not."

Vince disappeared inside the customs office. Long moments passed and still he didn't reappear. What could be keeping him? At last they saw him leave the customs building, smiling broadly, and come their way with an official.

"Hop out, kids! You've got some questions to answer."

Tom gave Liz a puzzled glance as they got out. The official consulted his clipboard, then studied their faces. "Where were you born?"

"Winnipeg."

"Bringing any goods into the USA?"

"No, sir."

"Staying more than twenty-four hours?"

"No."

After a few more questions, the official gave Vince's car a thorough examination. Then he nodded, and walked away.

"We did it," Vince exclaimed. "Let's get going."

Gunning the engine, Vince took the car out of the parking lot on smoking wheels.

"Is this really the USA?" Tom said, feeling disappointed as he looked at hotels and stores lining the wide streets. "It's just like Canada."

Vince smiled. "Could be, but it looks like home to me."

"Oh yeah, I forgot. You're from the USA."

Liz's grip tightened as the sports car swerved around a corner, then she frowned. "Are you an American, Vince? I didn't know that."

"Yeah, I'm from good old San Fran. I think that's the first place I'll visit, now I'm home again."

"But aren't you going back to Canada?"

"Sure, sure. I'm just talking about the extended holiday I'm planning."

Leaving the buildings behind, they drove into a park. This early in the year, the park was empty. The occasional person could be seen walking a dog, but otherwise the park was deserted as they followed a road toward a wide body of water.

"Is that the Niagara River?" Tom asked.

Vince nodded. "It flows through the rapids, then

drops over the falls. You see all those trees on the far side of the river? That's Canada."

Liz glanced at the river, then returned her puzzled gaze to Vince's face. "A park seems a strange place for an FBI office. Anyway, you could have phoned."

"You're right, Liz." Vince swung the wheel, and the car pulled to a stop behind a fast-food stand. No other vehicles were in the lot. "Wait here while I phone. Can I bring you something to eat?"

"A hot dog for me, please," Tom said.

Liz shook her head. "Nothing, thanks."

When Vince was gone, she rubbed her cheek thoughtfully. "Remember what I said about the discovery of the diamonds smelling like a very old egg? Well, my nose is twitching again."

"You think there's something strange about this trip?"

Liz nodded.

"Me too. I tell myself that Vince has been good to us, but another voice inside keeps asking a lot of questions. Like, if Vince really is a Mountie, why were we held up for so long by the customs officers at the bridge?"

"And here's another question: why are we the only customers at this stand? Can the food be that bad?"

"Either that, or it's closed."

"Then why hasn't Vince come back?"

"Maybe he's decided to swim to the FBI office."

"Anything seems possible with Vince." Liz opened the door. "Let's investigate."

A cold wind whipped up whitecaps on the river, and the bare branches of trees rattled as Tom and Liz cautiously approached the front of the stand and found it closed. A notice said, *See you in the summer!* There was no sign of Vince.

"So where is he?" Liz commented.

"In those woods, I think," Tom said nervously. "Look."

Someone was pushing toward them through thick bushes. As Vince stepped out, they glimpsed the roof of a parked vehicle. Then the bushes closed behind Vince, and he smiled.

"Got tired of waiting?"

Liz nodded. "What's happening, Vince? You're not really a Mountie, are you?"

"Don't you believe me?"

"We want to, Vince. But you're acting so strangely."

"O.K., my friends, it's time for the truth." Vince came forward, grinning, and put his hands on their shoulders. "You've been more help than you realize."

Liz smiled happily. "Well, that's good."

"Let's go for a walk while I explain."

Vince led them along a narrow path through the trees. "All truth-seekers, follow me," he exclaimed happily, trying to click his heels.

Tom gave his sister a worried look. "He's gone nutty, Liz," he whispered. "Let's turn back."

"I think he's harmless. A bit vain, but hardly dangerous."

The path ended abruptly. To one side a dirt road curved toward the place in the woods where Tom had noticed the parked vehicle; to the other side was open land sloping down to the river bank. A woman in a wheelchair sat on a small dock, watching the waves lap around the pilings.

As she turned and waved cheerfully, Tom gasped in surprise. "It's Tia!"

"Hi, there," she called. "Why'd you take so long?"

Vince smiled as they approached the dock. "They wanted to look behind the falls, so we went to Table Rock House. I figured one final treat wouldn't hurt, after all the help they've given us."

"I approve, Vince. Even young law-breakers deserve some fun."

Tom stared at Tia, trying to understand what she was saying. Then she reached under the cushion of her wheelchair, and his heart lurched as she produced a small pistol.

"Nobody move," Tia ordered. Her face was grim. "I'm not afraid to use this gun."

11

For a moment there was only silence.

Then a gull screamed over the river, and Tia chuckled. "Surprised, kids?"

"But . . . ?"

"What a moment of triumph. I'll remember it forever."

Suddenly Tom understood. On the path between the
dock and the woods there were two long tracks, identical
to those near the cabin where he'd been held prisoner.
They were the tracks of Tia's wheelchair.

"So, *you* were the driver of the van!"

Tia nodded, still chuckling. She looked at Vince.
"Tell him what happened, partner."

Vince smiled. "Remember refusing to say where
you thought the diamonds were hidden? I phoned Tia

and she arranged for the men to grab you on the streetcar. We wanted to learn your theory."

"So the diamonds *were* hidden in Sir Nigel's
shower?"

"Yes. As soon as you'd coughed that up, Tia phoned
from the cabin and I raced to Casa Loma. People were
used to me at the castle, so I wandered up to Sir Nigel's
bathroom and locked the door. In a few minutes the
main pipe was off, and I was holding a small metal tube
full of diamonds."

"No wonder the shower stopped working for me.
The water must have shifted the tube, and it blocked
the main pipe."

Vince started to speak, but Tia cut him off.

"I decided to hide fake diamonds in Sir Nigel's
desk. The old fool had shown me the false drawer."

"He's not an old fool," Liz protested. "He gave
you a job, and trusted you. It's terrible how you've
treated him."

Tia's cheeks turned red. "Be quiet, you."

"I won't be quiet. You're a thief and you should return
the diamonds immediately."

"But I don't have the diamonds, and neither does
Vince."

"What?"

Tia laughed. "That's shut you up. Now, as I was
saying, once the real diamonds were safely out of Casa
Loma, the chauffeur phoned your uncle with the tip to
look in Sir Nigel's desk. That discovery gave Vince
time to make preparations for the jewels to cross the
border."

"But you don't have the diamonds."

"*We* don't have them, but you do."

"*What?*"

Tia broke into delighted laughter. "If you could see your faces!"

Vince laughed too, but only briefly. "Come on, Tia. Time's a-wasting."

Suddenly she turned the gun his way. "I said *nobody* move. That includes you, partner."

"Are you crazy?"

"No, just greedy." Tia smiled. "I've been thinking, Vince. It's stupid to settle for a half-share, when all the diamonds could be mine."

"Why, you crook! You double-crosser!"

Vince's face turned dark with fury. He started toward Tia but her finger tightened on the trigger, and he stopped dead.

"That's right, partner. Take it easy, or you'll suffer severe lead-poisoning." Tia's eyes flicked toward the river, where a small motor boat with *Niagara Rentals* lettered on its sides was bobbing beside the dock. "Get in that thing."

"Why should I?"

"Because I had it specially delivered, just for your getaway. Soon you'll be across the river in Canada, and you can find a nice tree to hide in from the Mounties."

"What about the kids?"

"They're staying with me as hostages."

"Keep the diamonds, Tia, but let Tom and Liz come with me."

"Not a chance. Get in that boat."

Tia turned to Liz. "Take off your jacket."

"So that's it," Liz exclaimed. "I should have known."

Tia chuckled. "You're a clever young lady, but not clever enough. Give me the jacket!"

Reluctantly, Liz took off the splendid satin jacket and watched Tia tear at the Blue Jays crest. Finally it came apart, and a shower of diamonds sparkled into Tia's lap.

"Beautiful," Tia whispered softly, letting the diamonds run through her fingers. "What a treasure, and it's all mine."

"May I have my jacket back?"

"Sure." Tia pocketed the diamonds, then tossed the jacket back to Liz. "Now yours, Tom."

When the diamonds from Tom's crest were safely in her pocket, Tia aimed her gun at the motor boat. "It won't go far with a leaky hull, partner, so get travelling. Otherwise I'll try some target practice."

"You rat! You couldn't have pulled off this operation without me."

"Hogwash. I was the brains, and you were just hired help. Now take a ride. My finger is getting itchy."

Muttering angrily, Vince reached for the starter and the engine rumbled into life. On Tia's instructions, Tom went to release the boat's mooring lines.

"Sorry, kid," said Vince quietly. "I didn't like tricking you, but how else could I safely smuggle the jewels?"

"I wish we weren't staying with Tia. I'm scared she'll use that gun."

"She'd plug me in two seconds, but not a couple of kids." Vince glanced toward Tia, then dropped his voice even lower. "Say, good buddy, may I have your cap? I'm afraid I'll get sunstroke out on the water."

"But you'll be across the river in fifteen minutes."

"That's true. But it would be a good disguise."

From behind, Tia's wheelchair squeaked as she rolled closer. "You two quit whispering. Tom, step back so I can get a clear shot at that dude."

Looking frightened, Vince put the boat into gear. He started to speak to Tom, then heard the click of the gun's hammer and quickly accelerated. Foam and spray flew from the boat as it swept away from the dock.

Tia laughed. "Good riddance to bad rubbish," she called, then motioned at Tom and Liz. "Walk ahead of me into the woods. We're going for a nice ride."

As Tom started walking, he heard the motor boat drop speed. He glanced back quickly and saw that Vince had stopped outside gunshot-range, and was looking their way. Vince was waiting for them, if only they could escape from Tia.

Hoping to distract Tia, Tom started talking. "Was it the chauffeur who pretended I'd stolen his wallet?"

"Yes. Then he drove to the cabin after you'd escaped, to help search for you."

"Why'd you wear the ski mask in the van?"

"So I wouldn't be recognized."

Tom looked at Tia; the pistol rested in her lap while she turned the wheels of her chair. "Why'd you park in these woods?"

"So you wouldn't see my van when you arrived with Vince. Boy, you're certainly one for questions."

Straight ahead, a long branch dangled low across the narrow road. Tom grabbed the branch as he passed; when it was bent tight as a spring, he let go. The branch snapped straight back at Tia.

"Run, Liz," he shouted.

Tom plunged through the bushes, hoping desperately that Tia would not start shooting. He raced out of the trees with Liz and headed for the dock, waving to Vince.

With a roar of power, the motor boat leapt through the water toward them. "Hurry," Tom shouted. His heart was hammering, and he expected gunfire.

Approaching the dock, Vince slowed the engine and yelled. There was no time for the motor boat to stop; they would have to jump, and Tom tensed every muscle as he waited for the right second.

"Now," Liz cried.

Together, they jumped through the air and landed safely in the boat. For a moment Tom was winded, then he staggered up as the boat shot away from the dock.

"I did it," Vince yelled into the wind. "Victory!"

Tom tried to thank him for the rescue, but was ignored as Vince looked back at the shore, then started laughing. "Here come the cops! Right on time!"

Amazed, Tom heard the howl of sirens in the park. The van, with Tia at the wheel, burst from the trees. Then, with a screech of metal, it veered to the right and stopped in a cloud of dust. As police cars surrounded the vehicle, Tia raised her hands in surrender.

"Yahoo!" Vince was beside himself with glee. "What a sight! That'll teach the dirty double-crosser!"

"But what happened?"

Vince grinned. "From the start, I planned to trick Tia. I knew her van would be hidden in the woods. Before letting the air out of her wheels so she couldn't drive anywhere, I phoned the Mounties in Canada to say the diamond thief they wanted was in the USA, in Riverside Park."

Vince paused, chuckling.

"I knew it would take time for the message to get from the Canadian Mounties to the American FBI, and then to the local cops. Before they could reach the park I planned to grab the diamonds from you two, then leave Tia to be arrested while I made my getaway."

Tom looked at the spectacle of lights whirling on the police cars in the park. "Well, Tia is certainly under arrest. But you're still out of luck, Vince."

"How's that?"

"The police will recover the diamonds from Tia. You went to all that trouble for nothing."

Vince grinned happily. "You think I'm stupid? Don't forget, I never trusted Tia."

"I don't understand."

"Think about it, kids. If fake diamonds have been used once, why not twice? And where else have you got crests, besides on your jackets?"

Vince broke into delighted laughter. Then he seized the caps from their heads, and waved them happily. "You guessed it! Knowing Tia might try to double-cross me, I told her the diamonds would be in the jacket crests. Those I filled with fakes, and put the real diamonds in the crests on your caps. Wasn't that a fantastic plan?"

Liz shook her head. "You've also been lucky, Vince."

"Sure I'm lucky, but so what? We're halfway across this river already. I'll get away once we land. The

Mounties will never find me, and I'll be rich beyond my wildest dreams!"

Feeling betrayed, Tom looked unhappily at the man he'd liked and trusted. "When we were going with Tia to her van, I thought you were waiting to rescue us. But you only wanted the diamonds from our caps."

Vince flashed one of his charming smiles. "Don't take it hard, Tom. You're still my good buddy, and so is Liz."

She snorted. "Everything you say is a lie, Vince. You robbed your friend Sir Nigel, and left him to die in the stables."

"That old geezer deserved to die! He's got more money than the King of Siam, and he still hoarded the diamonds. Why didn't he give them to the needy?"

"The needy like you?"

"Sure like me! I'm just an ordinary guy struggling to make a living, and meanwhile Sir Nigel eats caviar in a castle. It made me sick, pretending to become his friend so I could worm out where he'd hidden the diamonds."

"Other people are greedy, but you're not?"

"That's enough backtalk, young lady. You like twisting things around so you can look smart."

"If you're not an undercover Mountie," Liz said, "then I bet Smythe is."

"Yes! I'll never forget his face when he was grabbed in the tunnel, and I made my getaway. Don't you see, the Mounties couldn't arrest and search me in Canada because they had no proof, so Smythe's job was to follow me until I tried to cross the border, then have the customs officers conduct a legal search for the diamonds."

"But they wouldn't have found them," Tom pointed out.

"Right again. I'm such an ace guy, I came up with the great idea of having you two carry the diamonds across the border. And you saw what happened. The customs officers searched me closely, but never thought to check you kids."

The motor coughed. Vince glanced at it, then whistled cheerfully as he turned his face to the sun. "I think I'll visit Florida to work on my tan."

The motor sputtered again and then cut out completely. Vince looked at the fuel tank. "It's empty! That double-crossing woman must have drained most of the fuel."

Liz smiled. "I guess she didn't trust you, Vince."

"Wipe that smirk off your face, and grab an oar! We're starting to drift."

Tom was surprised by the urgency in Vince's voice. Then he heard a sound that seized him with fear.

Whirling round, Tom looked downriver. "We're heading for the rapids!"

Liz grabbed an oar, and began paddling frantically. "Look what's beyond them!" she screamed.

In the distance, where the river appeared to end abruptly, a cloud of spray was rainbowed in the sunshine. It marked the deadly place where the river plunged over the falls to the rocks far below.

Seizing an oar, Tom tried to help Liz drive the boat to safety. But the current was strong, and carried the boat steadily toward the terrible booming of the rapids.

"It's hopeless," Vince shouted. "Drop those oars and hang on!"

A huge rock loomed straight ahead. Tom shut his eyes, then felt the surging water toss the boat away from the rock. Cold spray stung his face, and he cried out in fear.

The cry was lost in the thunder of the rapids and Tom could only stare helplessly at the white water leaping around jagged rocks. The boat veered past a huge boulder, then spun into a sickening whirlpool and as quickly whirled back into the roaring torrent.

Suddenly the rapids ended. Tom's grip on the boat loosened, but his relief was short-lived. He shook the spray from his face and saw that within seconds the ruthless water would carry them to the brink of the falls.

"That log," Vince screamed. "Grab that log when we hit it!"

Ahead was a log jammed between two boulders. Tom somehow managed to seize a branch as the boat hit the log. He pulled himself out of the boat—just before it was swept over the falls.

Stunned, Tom stared at the place where the boat had disappeared. Then he crawled higher up the log and his heart leapt with relief when he saw Liz and Vince.

"We're safe," Tom shouted above the deafening noise of the falls. "I can't believe it!"

"*Safe?*" Vince cried. "You call this *safe?*"

Water was churning angrily around the log. Tom shifted his position and the log trembled; with the weight of three people on it, the log was likely to break free at any second.

Filled with fear, Tom looked toward the shore. At Table Rock House, people stared and pointed. Only a short while ago, Tom had been safely standing there, joking about people who'd gone over the falls.

A tremor passed through the log, and the river foamed higher as if determined to tear it loose from the rock. Tom looked desperately at the crowd on shore, wishing they could somehow help.

Liz cried out and Tom's head snapped round toward the sound, afraid she had fallen in. But his sister was pointing at the sky.

"Look!"

Tom stared at a giant rescue helicopter. As the huge machine descended slowly out of the sky, he shouted with joy and relief.

"You see?" he called to Vince. "We really are safe!"

The man's face was pale with fear. His grip tightened as the whirling blades created a windstorm that shook the log. A hatch opened in the belly of the helicopter and a rescue basket dropped down. Vince glanced at the basket dangling beside him, then clung even tighter to the log.

"Hurry, Vince," Liz shouted. "Before it's too late!"

Tom saw terror in Vince's eyes. At any moment the log would break loose; Tom knew he must hurry. Moving carefully along the slippery log, he reached the basket and within seconds had been whirled to the safety of the helicopter, where he was wrapped inside a blanket.

But the danger was not over, and Tom's body shook as he watched the basket drop again to the log. "Hurry, Liz," he whispered, watching his sister crawl toward the basket.

Reaching it, she stopped to shout something to Vince. When he shook his head, Liz climbed into the basket; the helicopter's winch tightened and very quickly Liz was being bundled inside a blanket by a crew member.

Wiping water from her eyes, Liz looked at the woman aiding her. "Vince is afraid to let go," she called above the noise of the helicopter.

"I'll help him." The woman quickly assembled some equipment. "Vince Winter comes across so big and strong, but now we see the truth!"

"How come you know it's Vince Winter?"

"Oh, I've seen him lots of times on TV."

As she was lowered in the basket, Tom looked at the man operating the winch. "How'd you get here so fast?"

"This rescue chopper is based at Niagara Falls. People often get into trouble."

Tom looked through the hatch. The woman was standing fearlessly on the log, strapping a harness around Vince. Then she signalled to the winch operator, and the machine whined.

As the harness ropes tightened, the woman forced Vince to release the branches and he rose away from the log. Spinning slowly like a giant beetle, Vince Winter was lifted to the helicopter and deposited on the deck.

The woman followed Vince through the hatch, and quickly undid the harness. When he was free, Vince stumbled to a seat and dropped into it with a sigh of relief.

"I did it, kids," he said, raising a triumphant hand to show he was still clutching the baseball caps. "Despite all that, I saved the diamonds!"

"So what?" Tom replied. "You're heading for prison, and the jewels will go to Sir Nigel."

"Sure," Vince said eagerly. "But, don't you see, Sir Nigel will have to give me a big reward for saving his diamonds!"

As the helicopter lifted away from the falls, Liz wrapped the blanket tighter round herself and grinned. "Boy, Vince, you're better entertainment than a dozen dancing bears. Life won't be the same without you."

12

As the little plane tilted, Tom felt his stomach lurch.

For a few seconds the plane flew on its side, one wing pointing at the swift blue river below. Then, with a sickening tumble, it was upside down.

"I can't watch," Liz moaned through her hands.

The plane righted itself, then swept into a narrow canyon over a stretch of seething white water.

"The rapids," Sir Nigel said. "Just like I promised you."

Uncle Henry laughed. "Haven't you kids had enough rapids?"

"Yes," Tom exclaimed.

The plane skimmed low over the water, then the scene was suddenly replaced by the image of a man's gigantic face. As he talked about the need to live in harmony with Nature, Tom wiped his forehead and leaned back in his seat; he'd had enough thrills lately.

The *World of Nature* film ended, and the lights went up. Sir Nigel smiled. "Was it as good as I promised?"

"For sure! Is this really one of the world's largest movie screens?" Tom asked.

"So they say. I see all the shows here at Ontario Place, but I confess to sometimes missing the cinemas in London, England."

"What's Britain like, Sir Nigel?"

"It's marvellous. I'll take you for a visit someday. I'm sure we can find you a spare mystery to solve."

A few minutes later, the group left the theatre to wander around Ontario Place. Sir Nigel had invited everyone responsible for the recovery of the diamonds to return to Toronto during the summer as his guests. Dexter Valentine and his wife had also joined the party.

"Who's hungry?" Sir Nigel asked, leading the way to a Chinese take-out stand.

Later, laden with chop suey and egg rolls, they found benches with a good view of a lagoon and its procession of floating bands, pedal boats and other vessels.

"Impossible," Liz said, reading the message in her fortune cookie. "I thought you could believe these things."

"What's it say?"

"I'm about to lose my head over a handsome stranger."

Uncle Henry smiled. "Liz is always cool, calm and

collected. I'd love to see her lose her head."

Smythe lifted a sweet-and-sour sparerib with his chopsticks, but they slipped and red sauce spotted his shirt. "I'd better learn to operate these things before my next undercover assignment."

"What is it?" Tom asked quickly.

Smythe smiled. "That's a secret, but I can tell you it's a big change from being a butler."

"Can you tell us what happened to the original butler at Casa Loma?"

"Sure. He took a holiday at the request of the police, and I replaced him in order to investigate Sir Nigel's disappearance. I understand he'll be back at Casa Loma soon, along with the other servants like poor Hatfield. I must say he's welcome to the job!"

Uncle Henry looked at Smythe. "I still don't understand why you quit that day, and left me in the lurch."

Smythe tried again with the chopsticks, and more sauce splattered. "Do you recall showing me the diamonds you found in Sir Nigel's desk? When your back was turned, I tested their hardness and quickly discovered they were fakes, which meant the real diamonds had been removed from the castle."

"But why did you quit?"

"To shadow my chief suspect, Vince Winter. You see, I couldn't tell you the truth about the fake diamonds, in case word got to Vince and he went into hiding. The police wanted Vince to think his plan had succeeded, so we could nail him at the border-crossing with the diamonds."

"But the story was in the newspapers."

Smythe nodded. "But there was no publicity about

us trailing Vince Winter, only a mention of two American suspects."

Tom blushed. "Then I spotted you in the tunnel at Niagara Falls."

Smythe laughed. "By the time I got out of the tunnel and rushed to join the American police, your motor boat was heading for the falls. You can imagine how terrible I felt."

"Well, it all worked out fine in the end."

A flock of ducks skidded to a landing on the water, and Tom tossed some chow mein in their direction. Then the group walked toward the waterslide, where kids shrieked joyfully as they twisted down long plastic chutes to plunge into a pool.

"Speaking of Casa Loma," Smythe said, "it was Vince who found a couple of petty crooks to pose as a chauffeur and a blacksmith."

"You know," Tom said, "I should have realized that Vince and Tia were secretly their bosses."

"Why's that?"

"I'd seen the tracks of Tia's wheelchair at Fort York, then the same marks were on the driveway at the cabin where I was a prisoner. Another tip-off came at the phone booth on the country road, when the driver of the van didn't chase me. That meant the driver was Tia, who couldn't run because of her disability."

"But what about Vince?"

"At first I couldn't understand why I had been grabbed on the streetcar," Tom explained. "Then the blacksmith asked where the diamonds were hidden.

Who could have told him I had guessed? Only three people knew I had a theory."

Mrs. Valentine smiled. "My husband and I were two of them."

Tom nodded. "And Vince was the third."

"But we're Americans, like Vince and Tia. How could you tell we weren't the villains?"

"Two main reasons, Mrs. Valentine. First, because it was Vince who arranged for me to take the streetcar. He was setting me up for the grab."

"And the second reason?"

"When Hatfield disappeared from the study, Vince said he'd contact the police. But they never showed up—obviously because Vince didn't want them poking around."

Smythe shook his head. "Vince and Tia figured they had covered every angle, but there's always an unexpected event that makes a crime go wrong."

"Poor Vince," Liz said. "He won't like giving up his fancy clothes for prison stripes."

The group was drawn by loud cries from children coming from the distance. They stopped to watch the wild battles in the water-wars area and the foam swamp. Then they became aware of even louder screams coming from the distance.

"What's that?" Liz said.

Sir Nigel frowned. "It's coming from the stage, where they have the open-air shows, but I can't imagine what's happening. Nobody was screaming when I saw the Toronto Symphony there."

"Let's investigate!"

Hurrying toward the noise, they saw that all around the stage, police officers were struggling to hold back thousands of hysterical girls who were trying to reach a young singer.

"Big deal," Liz said. "It's a rock concert. Look at all those crazy girls, going gaga over some no-talent pretty face."

"It's somebody new," Tom said. "I've never heard of him before."

"How do you know his name?"

"It's on that sign. He's called Nick Nalini."

"*Nick Nalini!* Are you kidding me?"

"Nope. Read the sign for yourself."

Liz trembled. "It really is Nick Nalini! Why didn't someone tell me?"

Uncle Henry laughed. "But he's just some no-talent pretty face, Liz."

"Don't ever say that about Nick Nalini! He's the most perfect creature ever born, and he's *right here*!" Liz broke into a run and disappeared into the seething mass of fans.

Sir Nigel laughed. "The fortune cookie was right. Liz has lost her head over a handsome stranger, but I'm sure she'll survive the experience. I just hope her eardrums survive that music!"

"You know," Smythe said, "the blacksmith should have made you listen to Nick Nalini music in the stables. I'm sure you would have revealed the diamonds' hiding-place in no time."

Sir Nigel smiled. "You could be right. One's bravery has its limits."

Irene studied him thoughtfully. "I admire you, Sir Nigel. You really stood up to those crooks."

"I must say the admiration is mutual, my dear. Now, don't you think it's time for the others to learn your secret role in this affair?"

Irene nodded, then turned to Uncle Henry with embarrassed eyes. "I must apologize for letting you believe I was a maid at Casa Loma. You see, I was under strict orders not to reveal my true identity to anyone, including you."

"You mean you were never one of the servants?"

She shook her head. "I'm also a Mountie, and, like Smythe, I was at the castle as an undercover investigator."

For a moment there was silence, then Uncle Henry laughed with surprise and delight. "You had me completely fooled! I must say I was very surprised when you left Casa Loma without saying good-bye."

"I felt bad about that, but it was impossible to tell you why I was leaving. I couldn't risk having the truth leak to the people I was after."

"Who were they?"

"The blacksmith and the chauffeur. I'm happy to report we arrested them early this morning."

Uncle Henry smiled at Irene. "Hey, you're really something! How about having dinner with me tonight?"

"I'd love to."

Looking pleased, Uncle Henry turned to Tom with a wink. "When we get home to Winnipeg, nobody will believe everything that's happened to us. Especially if word gets out that it all ended with me dating a good-looking Mountie!"

Tom laughed. "Your secret is safe with me, Unc."

Eric Wilson at Casa Loma

This mystery was written early in Eric's career. Along with *Terror in Winnipeg* and *The Ghost of Lunenburg Manor* it is now available to fans of Eric Wilson Mysteries in a new edition featuring exciting illustrations by Susan Tooke.

TERROR IN WINNIPEG

A Tom Austen Mystery

ERIC WILSON

A stunning blast tore apart the gate.

Excitement explodes from the opening page in a thriller
that pits young Tom Austen against the evil genius of a
person whose real identity comes as a terrible shock. Don't
miss this action-packed read!

"I found this book electrifying! My favourite part was when
Tom sneaked into the DEMON apartment building and
got chased by the man with the white-streaked hair."
—*Justin H., Dartmouth, Nova Scotia*

VANCOUVER NIGHTMARE

A Tom Austen Mystery

ERIC WILSON

Tom tried to go lower but his foot slipped and dropped into open air. An electric shock of fear passed through him . . .

A chance meeting with a drug dealer named Spider takes Tom Austen into the grim streets of Vancouver's Skid Road, where he poses as a runaway while searching for information to help the police smash a gang that is hooking young kids on drugs.

Suddenly unmasked as a police agent, Tom is trapped in Vancouver's nightmarish underworld as the gang closes in, determined to get rid of the young meddler at any cost.

"Tom Austen has so much love and caring inside him."
—*Tara W., Pointe-Claire, Québec*

THE GHOST OF LUNENBURG MANOR

A Tom and Liz Austen Mystery

ERIC WILSON

"Would you like to visit a haunted house?"

While in Nova Scotia, Tom and Liz Austen are swept up in a series of spine-chilling events: a fire burning on the sea . . . icy fingers in the night . . . and a dog that suddenly won't go near its master's room!

"I enjoyed the excitement and I learned a lot. I've lived in Nova Scotia all my life and never knew what it meant when someone called me a Bluenoser."
—*Amanda N., Lower Sackville, Nova Scotia*

DISNEYLAND HOSTAGE

A Liz Austen Mystery

ERIC WILSON

The air was blasted by the huge rotors of a helicopter which roared in above the wall and hovered over the fort, shaking us with the force of the wind storm it created.

On her own during a California holiday, Liz Austen is plunged into the middle of an international plot when a boy named Ramón disappears from his room at the Disneyland Hotel. Has Ramón been taken hostage? Before Liz can answer that question, her own safety is threatened when terrorists strike at the most unlikely target: Disneyland itself.

"When I was reading *Disneyland Hostage* I forgot that a man wrote it. Eric Wilson really knows what girls think."
—*Melissa F., Trail, British Columbia*

THE EMILY CARR MYSTERY

A Liz Austen Mystery

ERIC WILSON

The spotlight swept back and forth, searching. I was freaked out of my mind!

Adventure and suspense await Liz Austen and her friend Tiffany in beautiful Victoria. After dangerous moments on dark ocean waters, the two are swept up in the strange world of the ancient Thirteen Oaks mansion and its troubled inhabitants.

"I would recommend this book to lots of people. Bravo!"
—*Hollis R., Victoria, British Columbia*

VAMPIRES OF OTTAWA

A Liz Austen Mystery

ERIC WILSON

Suddenly the vampire rose up from behind a tombstone and fled, looking like an enormous bat with his black cape streaming behind in the moonlight.

Within the walls of a gloomy estate known as Blackwater, Liz Austen discovers the strange world of Baron Nicolai Zaba, a man who lives in constant fear. What is the secret of the ancient chapel's underground vault? Why are the words *In Evil Memory* scrawled on a wall? Who secretly threatens the Baron? All the answers lie within these pages, but be warned: *reading this book will make your blood run cold.*

"I enjoyed *Vampires of Ottawa* a lot. Eric Wilson really had my mind going a couple of times!"
—*Alyson B., Perth-Andover, New Brunswick*

THE INUK MOUNTIE ADVENTURE

A Tom Austen Mystery

ERIC WILSON

The houses of the tiny hamlet seemed defenceless, huddled together under the roaring flames.

What is the sinister conspiracy code-named CanSell, and how does it threaten Canada? The truth is on a micro-cassette that Tom Austen must somehow find before a crucial vote is made by Canadians on the future of their country.

"This book is a page turner because anything can happen out of the blue! The characters make you wonder what they'll do next."

—*Matt C., Ottawa, Ontario*

THE GREEN GABLES DETECTIVES

A Liz Austen Mystery

ERIC WILSON

I almost expected to see Anne signalling to Diana from her bedroom window as we climbed the slope toward Green Gables, then Makiko grabbed my arm. "Danger!"

While visiting the famous farmhouse known as Green Gables, Liz Austen and her friends are swept up in baffling events that lead them from an ancient cemetery to a haunted church, and then to a heart-stopping showdown in a deserted lighthouse as fog swirls across Prince Edward Island. Be prepared for eerie events and unbearable suspense as you join the Green Gables Detectives for a thrilling adventure.

"I did a project on *The Green Gables Detectives* and got 95%. My favourite part was when Liz swallowed the oyster."
—*Paul H., Fortune, Newfoundland*